Maizy Chen's
LAST CHANCE

Maizy Chen's LAST CHANCE

LISA YEE

Random House 🏠 New York

Text copyright © 2022 by Lisa Yee
Jacket art copyright © 2022 by Rebecca Shieh

Photographs courtesy of: The Miriam and Ira D. Wallach Division of Art, Prints and Photographs: Picture Collection, The New York Public Library (p. 262); Prints & Photographs Division, Library of Congress (p. 267); Truckee-Donner Historical Society (p. 264); © Underwood Archives/Getty (p. 265); © Weegee (Arthur Fellig)/International Center of Photography/Getty Images (p. 266); all other photographs from the personal collection of Lisa Yee, used by permission.

Visit us on the Web! rhcbooks.com

Educators and librarians, for a variety of teaching tools,
visit us at RHTeachersLibrarians.com

Library of Congress Cataloging-in-Publication Data
Names: Yee, Lisa, author.
Title: Maizy Chen's last chance / Lisa Yee.
Description: First edition. | New York: Random House Children's Books, [2022]
Summary: "Eleven-year-old Maizy Chen visits her estranged grandparents, who own and run a Chinese restaurant in Last Chance, Minnesota; as her visit lengthens, she makes unexpected discoveries about her family's history and herself" —Provided by publisher.
Identifiers: LCCN 2021005416 | ISBN 978-1-9848-3025-8 (trade) | ISBN 978-1-9848-3026-5 (lib. bdg.) | ISBN 978-1-9848-3028-9 (ebook)
Subjects: CYAC: Grandparents—Fiction. | Restaurants—Fiction. | Chinese Americans—Fiction. | Immigrants—Fiction. | Racism—Fiction. | Genealogy—Fiction.
Classification: LCC PZ7.Y3638 Mai 2022 | DDC [Fic]—dc23

Printed in the United States of America
10 9 8 7 6 5 4
First Edition

For Mom and Dad, for Benny and Kait,
and especially for my grandparents, who made the journey

No story starts at the beginning.

Chapter 1

The pies were fake, but my grandparents didn't know that. Not at first, anyway. My mother had invited them to watch her work on a Tasty Flaky Pie Crust commercial. When I first started going with her to the set, Mom told me, "As a food stylist, my job is to make sure everything looks good for the camera."

Oma and Opa showed up directly from the airport wearing matching airplane pillows around their necks. My job was to make sure they didn't get into trouble.

My grandmother's luggage had barely touched the floor when she rushed over and, in her excitement, practically knocked me down. Oma's hug felt awkward partly because of the neck pillow and also because, even though I was eight years old, it was the first time I'd met her in person. My best friend thinks it's weird that I don't know my grandparents that well. Her family is really close.

"It's complicated," I've tried explaining to Ginger. But the truth is, I don't understand it myself. My mom and I talk about almost everything, but when it comes to her relationship with her parents, that's a different story.

On the set, Opa beamed brighter than the soundstage lights dangling overhead. "Maizy, you're so big!" my grandfather kept repeating before he got distracted by the pretend kitchen with only one wall.

That's when Oma pointed to a tight circle of people. "Shouldn't they be working?" she asked. "Why aren't they working?"

Mom stood calmly in the middle while the director yelled, "Charlotte, I need practice pies, now!"

"You'll get your pies," Mom said, motioning to the two-dozen pies lined up on folding tables.

Some were fully baked, others were ready for the oven, preparing for their close-ups. My grandparents watched in shocked silence as Mom's perfectly rounded scoops of mashed potatoes stood in for vanilla ice cream, since potatoes don't melt. Instead of milk, glasses were filled with glue because that looks better on camera.

Oma and Opa are in the food business, too. They own the Golden Palace. That's their Chinese restaurant in Last Chance, Minnesota. Mom once told me, "Maizy, you're the last of the Last Chance Chens." That seemed weird, since I'd never even been there.

I leaned in to eavesdrop as my grandparents began to whisper.

"Where did Charlotte learn that?"

"Not from us!"

"It's not real food."

When Mom topped the pies with a can of shaving cream instead of whipped cream, Oma looked like she had just seen a zombie.

It was all too much. My grandmother grabbed her suitcase with one hand, and my grandfather with the other. "Come on, we're going home!"

"But we just got here—" Opa protested. By now he had noticed that the back of the oven was missing and that there was a camera inside it.

Before he could say anything more, Oma kissed the top of my head. "We love you, Maizy. Come visit us!"

That was the last time I saw my grandparents. Until today.

Chapter 2

An elderly woman is sweeping the sidewalk with a bamboo broom.

"Oma?" I call to her.

My grandmother drops the broom and clutches her heart. The huge black bear sculpture that towers over her makes me nervous.

"Opa!" she cries into the Golden Palace restaurant. "Our Maizy has arrived!"

From inside, a man's shaky voice calls out, "Maizy? Maizy, come here so I can look at you!"

"My little Maizy," Oma says. This is ironic, since my grandmother is only a couple of inches taller than me. "You've finally decided to visit!"

I don't tell her I didn't have a choice. She looks much happier today than the last time I saw her, three years ago, on the Tasty Flaky set. That commercial landed Mom on the cover of *Food Stylists Monthly*, but what she remembers most about it is that her parents left without even saying hello.

A boy on a battered bike glides past, then circles around, slamming on his brakes. Doesn't he know it's rude to stare?

I tiptoe past the scary bear and hear my mother clearing her throat. She's leaning against our Honda with her arms crossed. An assortment of smashed bugs grace the windshield, casualties of our three-day road trip from Los Angeles.

"Hello, Mom." My mother lowers her sunglasses. "Maizy didn't drive herself to Last Chance. I'm here, too."

Chapter 3

When I step inside the Golden Palace, the smell of sautéed garlic and ginger reminds me that I haven't eaten in over two hundred miles and I'm starving! I look around in wonder. Red Chinese paper lanterns dangle from the tin ceiling. An old American flag with stars missing hangs near a fancy gold key displayed on the wall.

The restaurant is empty except for an ancient-looking lady sitting at the center table. She's watching us like we're a reality television show.

"Maizy, over here!"

I follow the sound of coughing. Near the kitchen, propped up in a wheelchair, is my grandfather. I smile, but his skinniness startles me. In the photos, he has a big belly.

Mom and Oma have emailed pictures back and forth for as long as I can remember, and we talk on the phone. We tried video chatting once, but it didn't go well. All my mother and I could see was the ceiling while Opa kept saying, "Is this on? How do you turn it on?" The emails and photos stopped a few months ago when their computer broke.

"Hey, Dad." My mother's voice is gentle. She kneels to talk to him. "How are you?"

"Fine! Good! Fit as a fiddle!" Opa grabs Mom's faded Dodgers cap. Her black hair tumbles down to her shoulders, making her look younger than she is. Opa's hair is silver, and even though he's in his eighties, he doesn't have many wrinkles.

"They make me sit in this dumb wheelchair all day just because they think I'm going to die soon." Opa winks at me.

Am I supposed to laugh?

Oma hugs me again. "Ignore that old goat!"

"Dad, really!" my mother protests. "You shouldn't say things like that."

We had so much fun driving cross-country, laughing nonstop and yelling out quotes from our favorite movies, like "Inconceivable!" from *The Princess Bride* and "There's no place like home" from *The Wizard of Oz*. But the closer we got to Last Chance, the quieter Mom became. She didn't even talk the last hour. My grandfather is the reason we're here.

"How are you feeling?" Mom asks.

Opa's eyes slowly shut. His body jerks. What do I do?! I turn to Oma, who says, "Maizy, you look hungry. Are you?"

"Call an ambulance," my mother shouts. "Dad, speak to me!"

"What?" He opens one eye, then the other, and says to Mom, "Gotcha, Charlotte!" Opa grins at me, and I find myself grinning back, even though my mother is not.

In the middle of the chaos, a customer walks in.

Oma hurries over and hands the man a red menu. Some of the letters have worn off, so the front reads: *olden Pal ce.*

"Is this authentic Chinese?" The big man loosens his tie and deflates.

My grandmother nods. "Absolutely! All our dishes are from ancient Chinese recipes."

"Good!" He shuts the menu. "Bring me chop suey and those cream cheese wontons. Chinese food has to be the real deal, or why even bother, right?"

Chapter 4

Oma motions for me to follow her into the kitchen. Fat bags of rice, boxes of fortune cookies, and gigantic jugs of soy sauce rest on metal shelves.

"Chop suey," she says, snorting. "That's not real Chinese food." She stops to hug me again. "Maizy!"

My grandmother reaches for a giant cleaver. I flinch, then marvel, as she dices pork, celery, and mushrooms with lightning speed. Using the sharp edge of the blade, Oma slides everything into a hot wok with minced garlic sizzling in oil. The flames roar so high I leap back. The smell makes my mouth water.

She pivots like LeBron James, dunking wontons into the deep fryer. Magically, they morph from white to a golden brown. Oma hands me one to munch on as she slides the chop suey from the wok onto a heavy white plate. I'm worn out just from watching her.

I fan my mouth. "I've never heard of cream cheese wontons before." It's sooo good—crispy on the outside, smooth and creamy on the inside.

"Dairy products are big in Minnesota," she explains, arranging the plates of food on a big, round black tray.

"So are these Chinese or American?" I ask.

"Yes," Oma answers.

Once the customer is fed, she cooks for me and Mom while Opa shares a cup of tea with the ancient lady.

"Maizy, sit," Oma insists. "It's time to eat."

We feast family-style on platters of chow fun noodles with char siu—barbecue pork—and fried rice with shredded omelet, snow peas, and curls of carrots. Steam rises from the spicy braised eggplant with minced pork.

I'm so hungry, but when I pick up the noodles with my chopsticks, they end up on my lap instead of in my mouth. "Oma, may I have a fork, please?"

"Chinese food should be eaten with chopsticks!" she says. I feel myself shrinking until she winks and slips me a fork. "Don't tell Opa!"

After we finish eating, I explore the restaurant, leaving Mom and Oma to talk in loud, angry whispers.

"It took you long enough to get here."

"I drove as fast as I could without getting a ticket."

"No, I mean it took almost thirty years."

I can't believe we came all this way just for them to argue. My mom almost never gets upset—but when she talks to Oma or Opa, her voice can get tense. I distract myself by looking at the pictures and memorabilia that cover the Golden Palace's walls. It's like a museum in here, only with tables, mismatched chairs, and food instead of art. Wait.

Mom tells people she works in the culinary arts—so maybe food *is* art, after all.

A faded photograph of a young Chinese bride is in a silver frame. A Golden Palace menu advertises full meals for fifteen cents. A poster of Hawaii seems out of place.

I wander into the little office off the kitchen. There's a pile of bills stacked on the desk and photos tacked up on the wall. Dozens of them, all of Chinese men. The people in the pictures look young, but the photos are really old. Tucked in a corner is a handwritten note. It's so faded I can barely read the words: *I am a Chinese American.*

"Come on, Maizy. Let's go get settled." Mom sounds weary.

The boy on the bike is still outside. We eye each other but don't say anything.

Oma makes a *tsk* sound when she spots the fast-food wrappers littering the floor of our car. "The house is unlocked. Do you know how to get there?"

My mother releases a sigh that's been building ever since we left California, or maybe even before. "I used to live there, remember?"

Chapter 5

It seems like the engine just started and already we're pulling up to a white house with a red door. Our neighbors, the Zangs, have a red door, too. Chinese people think red is good luck.

While Mom is wrestling with our luggage, I grab a bag and dash inside. All the furniture looks comfy but old. Our house is really trendy, and we even have an expensive designer couch that no one's allowed to sit on. Here, there's a painting of dogs playing poker in the living room, and all the photos on the wall going up the stairs are of me. When I get to the top, I'm faced with my most recent school picture—the one where I refused to smile because of my braces. Dork.

A handwritten sign on a door warns, *KEEP OUT OR ELSE!* I take my chances. Mom's room doesn't look like the rest of the house. The purple dresser matches the purple canopy bed. One patch of wall has puffy stickers all over it. My mother would kill me if I put up stickers in my room.

There's a red typewriter on the small desk. The bookshelves are crammed with Judy Blume paperbacks and *Mad* magazines. A prom photo is on the bulletin board. Mom's got frizzy hair and is standing next to a boy with a goofy smile. The two of them look deliriously happy, like they're sharing a secret.

"Asian perm." Mom drops my suitcase next to the beanbag chair. "I wanted to look like all the other girls with their curly hair, but my hair rebelled. Maizy, you can stay in my room."

"Really? I'd love to!"

Mom picks up an old Polaroid camera. "Smile!"

We're both surprised when it flashes and spits out a photo. She hands me the Polaroid, and I watch my image slowly come into focus.

"Honey, there's something I need to tell you."

I hold my breath. Whenever people say they "need to tell you something" instead of just saying it, it's never good.

My mother looks down at her hands. "Opa is much sicker than I realized."

When Mom got the phone call from Oma, I could hear her crying. "Why didn't you tell me? Why did you wait?"

That was last Wednesday. On Thursday, Mom rearranged her work schedule and canceled my summer camp. By Friday, we were on the road. Today is Sunday.

Apparently, Opa had been sick for a while, but they didn't tell us until last week because Oma didn't want to be a bother—and Opa didn't want anyone to know. Ginger's abuela loves to share every little ache and pain and has been known to make up a few. In my family, sometimes what's not said takes up more space than what is.

"How sick is he?" I ask. Other than the wheelchair and being so skinny, Opa seems fine. He laughs and jokes a lot. Would someone who's really sick do that?

Mom flops onto the bed and talks to the ceiling. "I'll be the one taking him to the doctor so I can get some solid information. It's impossible to pry a straight story out of your grandmother. I'm sure he'll get better soon enough."

"Like in a week? Two weeks?"

"More like a month, maybe even two months. Maizy, I honestly don't know. It'll be an adventure!" My mother sounds cheerful and looks worried. She's always been excellent at multitasking.

Two months? Wait! That's almost the whole summer. I'm supposed to have fun during vacation, not be stuck in Last Chance. I know I should feel bad for Opa, but the person I'm feeling most sorry for is myself.

Chapter 6

'm in the living room. Pill bottles sit on a table that's already crowded with a couple of decks of cards and a clear box filled with colorful poker chips. Sheets, a blanket, and pillows are folded neatly on the couch. Opa sleeps in here, since he can't make it up the stairs and Oma can't carry him.

"I might be stuck here all summer!" I wail into my phone.

"Maizy, how will I get through the brunches without you?" Ginger asks.

Every Sunday, all the Ortega relatives gather at Ginger's abuela's house for a huge potluck. Ginger's got so many cousins that some even have the same first names. I wish I had a big family. Her mom has lots of brothers and sisters and in-laws, plus there will be even more relatives when she gets remarried next year. My mother hasn't even been married once.

After my call, Mom suggests I explore the town. So far it's pretty boring. They don't even have a movie theater. I'll bet nothing ever happens in Last Chance.

Back home, houses practically lean against one another.

Here, there are big front lawns and plenty of space in between homes. Everything looks old. I stop to gawk at a spooky gray mansion. The weeds are really tall, and the fountain is dry. I assume the house is abandoned, until I see lace curtains part ever so slightly. Creeped out, I hurry away.

Main Street goes on for three blocks and dead-ends at the Last Chance Lutheran Church. Nearby, I smell something wonderful. *The world's best bratwurst!* is painted on the window. I take a photo of the Werner's Wieners sign to show Ginger. That'll crack her up.

A big dog is motionless on the sidewalk. Is he dead? I tiptoe toward him, and to my relief, his eyes open. He lets out a yawn.

I lean down to pet him. "Hello," I say. "I'm Maizy."

He's got chocolate-brown fur with a heart-shaped patch of white on his forehead. They say that dogs can't smile, but this one sure looks like he's smiling back at me.

Last Chance Bank & Library sounds interesting. I try the door, but it's locked. On a tiny yellow Post-it, in curly hand-writing, someone has written, *Closed due to flood. For deposits or withdrawals, call Daisy G.*

There's no phone number.

I spot the Last Chance Bait 'n' Tackle down a side street. The shop also sells life insurance. It seems like everything here is also something else. I wonder what the Golden Palace doubles as.

When I near the Ben Franklin Five & Dime and Soda Fountain, a lady opens the door as if she's been waiting for me. Her name tag reads: *Eva*. With her shock of short white hair, I can't tell if she's old or young.

"So good to see you again!" Eva says.

"Um, it's my first time here."

She squints through her rhinestone glasses. "Oh, silly me. You look like someone else."

I always thought I looked like myself.

"So, where are you from, hon?"

"California."

Eva shakes her head. "I mean, where are you *from?*"

"Los Angeles—"

"Your people, your nationality."

Ooooh. Okay.

"My nationality is American," I say. But then, because I know what she's really asking, I add, "But my race, if that's what you mean, is Chinese."

"Well, welcome to Last Chance. You should try the Golden Palace. Best Chinese food in Minnesota!"

I smile weakly. Ginger and I have been talking nonstop since we met in first grade, but I've never been good at talking with strangers.

The Ben Franklin Five & Dime smells like apples. The handcrafted jewelry and glass jars crammed with colorful candies make me feel like I've walked into a treasure chest. A big, bald man in a nubby orange sweater sits at the soda fountain counter. He looks up from his banana split, but when our eyes meet, he turns away, almost shyly.

Later, I head to the checkout counter and hand Eva a

butterfly barrette. She nods. "I was wondering who this belongs to." Then Eva gives me the 15 percent off Friends and Family discount even though we've just met.

There's a train depot at the edge of downtown. When I peer through the window, all I see is dust and cobwebs, like the place has been deserted for decades. Across the way, there's an old stone well that could be right out of a fairy tale. I hope there aren't any evil villains in Last Chance. I know! I'll send Ginger a video of me making a wish, just like Snow White in the movie.

I pull out my phone, lean over the edge of the well, make my wish, and . . .

Chapter 7

"Nooooooo!"

Mom has warned me a million times that if I lose my phone again she isn't buying me a new one. I keep pacing around the well, as if that can help.

"Hi!" The boy who was hanging around earlier rides up on his bike. "I'm Logan! Did you just make a wish? I've got tons of wishes down there. One time I wished for a llama. . . ."

The trail of light brown freckles marching across his nose match his hair color. Logan seems to enjoy talking to strangers as much as I hate it. I wait for him to take a breath so I can ask, "Would you mind calling me?"

Logan looks surprised.

"I mean, can you call my cell phone? It fell in the well, and I want to see if it still works."

"It's probably broken," Logan says matter-of-factly. "But sure, I can call you."

He takes a pen out of his pocket and writes my number on his hand. "What's your name? Why are you here? Where are you from?"

No one in LA ever asks me where I'm from.

Logan's annoying, but I need his help. "My name is Maizy, I'm visiting my grandparents, and my ancestors are Chinese."

He nods. "Uh. Okay. Sure. But where are you from, though? Like Saint Paul? Madison? You know, what city?"

Oh! "I'm from Los Angeles."

"Disneyland," Logan whispers with awe before riding away.

"Wait!" I yell after him. "I thought you were going to call me?"

"I will," he cries over his shoulder. "I don't have a cell phone, so I'll call you from home. Bye, Chinese American Maizy from Los Angeles!"

Chapter 8

Yesterday I waited forever at the wishing well and Logan never called. Or maybe he did and that means my phone is broken. I haven't told Mom yet.

When I arrive at the Golden Palace for lunch, I'm greeted by the wooden bear. He's about two feet taller than me. I raise my hands up like claws and let out a loud growl.

"Maizy!" Opa rolls to the door in his wheelchair. "I see you've met Bud. He won't bite. Shake his hand!"

Embarrassed to have been caught growling, I pat the bear's paw.

Inside, the ancient-looking lady from yesterday is at the same table in the middle of the restaurant. "You there!" She locks her ice-blue eyes on me so tight I can't move. "Do you work here, little girl?"

"Me?" Even though she's half his size, this lady is scarier than Bud the Bear.

Oma appears at my side. "Lady Beth, what can we get for you?"

The old woman turns a bowl upside down. "Empty!"

"Maizy," Oma tells me, "more fried wonton strips for Lady Beth, and a fresh pot of tea."

Lady Beth gifts us with a thin smile. "How is my ginger eggplant coming along?" Her voice is sticky sweet when she talks to my grandmother.

"We will check on that immediately," Oma promises. Hands on my shoulders, she marches me into the kitchen, whispering, "Lady Beth is the richest person in town."

Is that supposed to be an excuse for bad behavior?

My mother is talking to a young woman with a nest of red hair. They are both staring at a giant purple eggplant like it's about to hatch.

"Charlotte! Daisy!" Oma barks. "Stand back."

She grabs a cleaver and slices the eggplant faster than the black belts in the Samurai Kitchen Knife commercials. The second Oma's done, she places a bowl of fried wonton strips in my hand and a pot of hot tea in the other. "For Lady Beth." She pushes me toward the dining room.

Mom huffs. "You mean Lady Macbeth? I call her that because she's such a drama queen. She used to order me around. Guess it's your turn now, Maizy."

The young woman's jaw drops. "Your name is Maizy? My name is Daisy!"

I wonder if she's the Daisy from the bank/library. How many Daisys could there be in Last Chance?

"Our names rhyme," Daisy is saying excitedly. Her necklace is made of colorful buttons. "It's like we're sisters or cousins, or relatives."

I nod, unsure of whether to tell her it doesn't work like that.

Back in the dining room, I cautiously approach Lady Macbeth.

"The tea?" she demands. Speechless, I pour and miss the cup. "Hmmmphhh," Lady Macbeth sniffs, as if I did it on purpose. Frantically, I mop up the mess with a napkin. I look for Mom to rescue me, but she's busy hugging some stranger.

"How long has it been, Charlotte?" His T-shirt says: *Reading Is My Superpower.*

Is she blushing? I think she's blushing.

"About one hundred years?"

They both burst out laughing, even though her joke isn't funny.

Neither has looked at me, but I can't stop staring at him. Wait—that goofy grin. He's the boy in the prom photo!

Since my mother's distracted, now's my chance. . . . "Hi, Mom, I may have dropped my phone down a well—okay, see you later!"

I'm almost out the door when I hear, "Come back here right now, young lady!"

Mom looks mad and amused. "Glenn, this is my daughter, Maizy. Maizy, this is my old friend Glenn Holmes—Principal Holmes now."

"Nice to meet you, Maizy." He shakes my hand. "I get the feeling that you're on the cusp of a mother-daughter talk, so that's my cue to exit. Charlotte, I'll catch you later."

"You'd better!" she calls after him, looking all fluttery.

Chapter 9

After our talk, where Mom did 100 percent of the talking, I wander into the kitchen. Oma is in the office shuffling bills. "Money, money, money," she keeps saying. "Everything costs money."

"True," I tell her. I'm going to have to pay for a replacement phone, and it's going to be so expensive. I look around the office walls again. "Who are those people?" I point to the old photos. My ancestors, maybe? Ginger's favorite Aunt Olive (she has two) traced their family back to Mexico in the 1800s. But I don't know anything about my family's history.

Oma bolts from the desk and yells, "Too much sugar!" startling Daisy, who spills it all over the counter.

Mom says that when my grandmother doesn't want to talk about something, she'll change the subject. Maybe Opa will tell me about those photos.

It's way past lunchtime now. The dining room is empty except for Lady Macbeth. "We eat at off-hours," Opa explains as Oma keeps bringing us more and more dishes. How hungry does she think we are?

Silently, my grandmother places a pair of chopsticks next to my plate. I put my fork down and attempt to use them. When a piece of orange chicken falls onto my lap, I scrunch it into my napkin. Only Lady Macbeth sees me. She shakes her head. I ignore her and move my chair to be closer to Opa.

Chapter 10

There's not a lot to do here. I miss Ginger. I've been in Last Chance for almost a week, and my closest friend is Opa—and he's in his eighties. My mother asked me to keep him company. Not that my grandfather isn't fun. But all he wants to do is be at the Golden Palace, and Mom wants him to spend more time at home, where he can rest.

"What's this?" He eyes the cards I put in front of him.

"I was hoping you'd teach me how to play poker."

Opa shakes his head. "I haven't played in three years."

"What's the matter? Afraid I'll beat you?" I say, grinning.

A playful look lights up his face. "Go get the poker chips. . . ."

There are so many rules! I search for something I can use to write them all down, but the only thing I can find is a blank *Guest Check* pad for taking customers' orders. That'll do. We each start with five cards in the game he's teaching me, but you can swap some of them out. Then you bet on your "hand," the combination of cards you have, and the goal is to win all the poker chips.

"It's not just the cards you're dealt. It's what you do with them that matters most," Opa tells me.

After about an hour, we take a snack break. Opa holds up a fortune cookie. He loves them so much that I brought a whole box home. "The kind wrapped in foil are more expensive, but classy."

"Last year, Mom and I went to a fortune cookie factory in San Francisco," I tell Opa. "They ride on a conveyor belt. Then someone puts a fortune in the middle of each cookie and shapes them by hand while they're still warm."

I fold a napkin to show Opa.

He nods with approval. "Hardly anyone in China eats them, but Americans expect them when they go to Chinese restaurants. They think they're good luck!"

"Are they?"

Opa winks. "They are if you want them to be."

"Have you ever been to San Francisco?"

He munches on another cookie. "Nope. Oma and I didn't travel. Couldn't leave the restaurant. Who'd run it while we were away?"

Is this why they only visited that one time?

My mother and Oma are finally home. They leave their shoes by the front door, where sweaters and Opa's fishing vest hang, before saying hello and returning to their argument. Distracted, Oma means to drape a blanket over Opa's shoulders, but instead it covers his head.

"Charlotte, you couldn't wait to get away, and to do what? Make fake food?"

Mom winces.

I look over at Opa, who has finally freed himself from the blanket.

"My work is in Los Angeles. They don't shoot commercials in Last Chance. I'm a food stylist," my mother says through gritted teeth.

From the look on Oma's face, she might as well have said, "I'm a pepperoni pizza."

Even though today's argument probably started minutes ago, it's clear it's been years in the making.

Mom's jaw tenses. "My clients are some of the biggest brands in America. What I do is considered art. I'm the one who styled the french fries for the new McDonald's commercial!"

"French fries?" Oma looks like she's just bitten into a lemon. "That's not real food."

I don't know. I always thought potatoes were food.

As they continue fighting, Opa puts the blanket back over his head.

Chapter 11

On Thursdays, hot fudge sundaes are half price. I'm back at Ben Franklin watching Eva top the whipped cream with crushed Nut Goodie—a candy bar made of chocolate, peanuts, and maple nougat.

I've brought one of my mother's old *Mad* magazines to read. Is this where she got her sense of humor from? Mom hasn't laughed much since we got to Last Chance, but she can be pretty funny. One time Ginger and I were using Mom's eyeliner to draw mustaches on each other when she caught us. "Maizy! Ginger! Put that down." We froze until she said, "For mustaches, use an eye shadow pencil. It'll go on smoother." Then she drew one on her face to show us.

Three girls about my age are sitting at the far end of the soda fountain. One is complaining to another, "I think my eyelashes are too long." The third girl looks bored. She's beautiful, like YouTube-star beautiful, with long blond hair. I'll bet she's stuck-up.

"I heard she's from Los Angeles."

Huh? Are the other two girls talking about me? Do they know I can hear them, or is that the point?

"Probably thinks she's better than us, right, Riley?"

The pretty girl doesn't answer.

One of the Mean Girls pulls her eyelids back.

The other is laughing. "You're too funny, Caroline!"

My face feels like it's on fire. Why is it that they're the ones being mean and I'm the one who feels embarrassed? Even though I've only just started my sundae, I get up to leave.

"Aw, she can't even take a joke," Caroline says.

I'm in such a hurry, I almost knock Logan over on his way in. "Hi, Maizy!"

I don't stop to talk. I need to get out of here, fast.

Oma motions toward the dirty-dishes cart. "Start with number eight." Every table in the restaurant has a number.

I fill the gray plastic bin as fast as I can. Using leftover tea, the way I've seen my mother do, I scrub the glass tabletops until they squeak. When all the dirty tables are clean, I feel better.

I go into the kitchen looking for Oma. "I love your dress," I tell Daisy. It looks like something you'd see at a retro flea market in LA. "Did you make it?"

She blushes and points to the shelf where we store the rice. "Thanks, Maizy. I used the rice bags."

"Where's Mom?" I ask when I find Oma back in the office.

"She took Opa to the doctor." My grandmother is tallying up the receipts without a calculator. "He's got a little cough. Your mother is worried. He's fine. There's nothing wrong with him."

If there's nothing wrong with Opa, why are we still here?

I look at the photos on the wall. Customers? Friends? Relatives? I like the ones that are old and faded, like ghosts. Some have names written under them: *Jack, Monty, Frank.* Each person is staring straight at the camera, right at me.

"Who are all of you?" I wonder. Now every time I come to the Golden Palace I visit them, like they're old friends. I'm about to ask Oma about the man who's holding up a heavy rice bag when Daisy peeks in from the kitchen. "Look, Maizy, I'm cooking!" She waves two fistfuls of scallions.

Oma shakes her head. She doesn't wear any makeup but still looks pretty with her short gray hair. Today a butterfly barrette keeps the bangs off her face. I have one just like it. I look at it a little closer—I think it *is* mine!

"I can't do everything by myself." Oma nods toward Daisy, who disappears from view. "She started when Opa first got sick. But that was before I knew her head is about as empty as a balloon."

"I can help, too," I tell my grandmother.

She kisses my cheek. "Maizy, you're a good girl."

Oma is so nice to me. Why can't she and Mom get along?

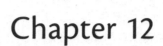

Chapter 12

I'm still in the office, practicing shuffling cards. I carry one of Opa's packs with me all the time. Mom finally shows up when I've just mastered the riffle. That's where you hold half a deck of cards in each hand and then bend the edges so they overlap each other when you release them.

"How's Opa?" I ask, setting the cards aside.

"He's at home resting." She brings her fingertips to her forehead. Mom does this when she has a headache. "The doctor says it would be better if he stayed home instead of coming to the restaurant every day." Oma keeps wiping the counter, pretending not to listen. "Too much excitement is bad for him."

Daisy is making dumplings and talking to herself. "Fill and fold, fill and fold, fill and fold—"

Mom rummages through the desk drawers looking for aspirin. "You okay, Maizy?" She can always tell when something is wrong.

"Some girls made fun of me," I mumble.

I'm embarrassed that I'm still upset—and I don't even

know those girls. Why is it that when someone is mean, you remember that much more than when people do nice things?

Daisy joins us. "People are the worst," she says.

Oma walks by with a tray of hot egg rolls. Mom reaches for one. "I'm off to take food to Opa," she says while munching.

"Let me," I volunteer. "I can stay with him, too."

My mother nods. "He'd like that."

For once Oma agrees with her. Before I leave, my grandmother whispers, "You're better than the bullies."

Chapter 13

I'm hardly five steps out of the Golden Palace when Logan's bike skids around the corner so fast he almost falls off. He slows as he follows me.

"What?" I snap, sounding harsher than I mean to.

Logan's smile slips off his face for a split second. "Here, you left it at Ben Franklin."

It's the *Mad* magazine. Before I can thank him, Logan pedals away.

I feel awful. This time I'm the mean girl.

When I get home with dinner, Opa's watching an overly cheerful man named Giancarlo "Carlos!" Franco, "your guide to America's small towns' biggest tastes." How can anyone eat soup while wearing a white suit?

"Yes!" Opa agrees with Carlos! "Soup is underrated. At the Golden Palace we serve wonton soup, hot and sour soup, egg drop soup . . ."

Carlos! is sitting in a café in Doylestown, Pennsylvania.

He points to the bowl of pepper pot soup and yells, "Delish dish!" with a level of enthusiasm usually reserved for football touchdowns.

"Darn doctor told me to stop watching so much news," Opa complains. "She claims it causes me stress. Maizy, you know what causes me stress? That doctor."

When Opa sees the takeout containers stamped with red pagodas, he jokes, "Chinese food again?"

Maybe he's sick of Chinese food and that's why he's eating less these days?

"Next time I can get something from town—maybe Werner's Wieners—" I offer.

"NO!" Opa shouts. "Nothing from Werner. Ever."

"Is his food that bad?"

Opa waves a hand dismissively. "His food is great, but don't ever tell him I said that. We don't discuss Werner in this house."

He turns back to Carlos!, who's saying, "A menu is like a story—appetizer, entrée, dessert! Beginning, middle, and a happy ending!"

"I love stories," I say. I try picking up my tomato beef chow mein with chopsticks. I'm getting a little better, but the noodles keep slipping off. "Opa, who are all those people on the wall in the office?"

"People on their way home." He opens his fortune cookie but doesn't eat it. He only nibbled on his lunch, too. " 'Run, don't walk,' " he reads, then laughs. "I'd be happy to be able to just stand."

"Last Chance couldn't have been our ancestors' first home. How did our family end up here?" I think about *The Wizard of Oz*. Dorothy's house was picked up and carried away by a tornado.

"Our story will probably bore you." He watches with amusement when I stab a wonton with one of the chopsticks and eat it like a shish kebab. "You're not interested in stuff like sailing ships, outlaws, and a gold mountain, are you?"

My mouth is full, but that doesn't stop me from saying, "Yes, I am!"

"Oh, all right, you twisted my arm." Opa reaches for a glass of water and with each sip sits up taller and looks more lighthearted. "Now, imagine yourself on the other side of the world. It's over a hundred and fifty years ago, when China was ruled by starvation and fear. But on one cold winter's night, there was a spark of joy—"

Already I can tell this is going to be a good story.

The Beginning

1853

Long ago in China, warlords ravaged the countryside. No one was safe, and millions of lives would be lost. But in a tiny village in Guangdong Province, a baby was born. His parents cried happy tears at the sight of their son, and their young daughter marveled over her baby brother.

Not everyone was pleased. From a dark corner of the hut, a gravelly voice complained, "Just another mouth to feed. Well, at least it's a boy. They are worth more than girls."

When she heard her old uncle, the new sister hung her head in shame, for she knew it to be true. Sons were cherished because they grew up to support their elders. Daughters were a burden to be married off to other families.

When the father wondered out loud what to name his new son, the sister looked at the crying baby. He was so little. "We are lucky to have him," she said. "Let's call him Lucky."

Years later, when the war finally ended, people were still poor. By then, the village had lost half its population, including Lucky's old uncle and big sister. The boy grew up alongside his father working in the fields. Crops were scarce, and the family often went hungry. However, when there was food, Lucky loved watching his mother cook.

Skinny but strong, Lucky was well liked by all. At the market, he never tired of listening to the villagers gossip. But the stories Lucky loved the most were about a wondrous place where men could help themselves to mountains of gold. In America, no one ever went hungry.

"My grandson sailed across the sea to search for the Gold Mountain," one elder boasted. "He found the Gam Saan and now sends us money every month."

"America is real?" Lucky asked, surprised.

The man pulled a shiny gold nugget from his pocket and held it up high. "America is as real as this!"

In that moment, Lucky knew his destiny.

Chapter 14

It's been days since I learned about Lucky. I can't wait to hear more, but Opa insists, "Good stories, like a good meal, should never be rushed. In time, you'll know the whole story," he explains as he pulls back the curtains to let the sunshine in.

The next day I'm still wondering, of all the places in America, how did Lucky end up in Last Chance?

"There's a lot to tell, but we'll get to it in due time," Opa reminds me.

"You said that yesterday, too, and the day before, and the day before!"

My grandfather laughs. "This is Last Chance, not Los Angeles. Around here we're not in any hurry."

Mom took Opa to see the doctor again. Both came home exhausted. Opa has heart disease. This makes Oma mad. "That's absurd 'cause that man's got the best heart of anyone I know!"

Opa is napping when I leave for the Golden Palace. I pat Bud's paw. I can't believe I was ever scared of him. I guess I just wasn't used to seeing bears. Mom is standing near the kitchen with Principal Holmes. Today's T-shirt says: *Book Nerd*. Whenever he shows up, which is all the time, she drops whatever she's doing to talk to him. I don't think he should be bothering her when she's trying to work.

Daisy hands me Opa's dinner. "Well, what do you say?!"

"Thank you?"

"They're new!" Daisy points to the paper to-go bag and lowers her voice. "Plastic bags can take over a thousand years to decompose." She perks up and adds, "I talked your grandmother into getting these recyclable ones."

When I tell her "That's great!" Daisy beams so bright that I practically have to shield my eyes. It's funny how one insult can ruin your day or how one compliment can make someone so happy.

I'd love to stay, but I need to get back to Opa. My job is to babysit. No one has used that word, but that's pretty much what it is. Mom says she'll pay me to stay with Opa. I don't tell her that I'll do it for free. It's so weird. A few months ago I had a babysitter. Now I *am* one, for a senior citizen.

"Maizy?"

"Hey, Opa, did you have a nice nap?"

"Refreshed and ready for poker before dinner!"

It takes a while for Opa to sit up. I know better than to try to help. We've been playing five-card draw. If you don't like the cards you're dealt, you can trade some for new ones.

"Your five cards have to work together," Opa explains. "It's like cooking Chinese food, where there are five main tastes—sour, sweet, bitter, spicy, and salty. Together, in balance, these create winning dishes. And if you get the right mix of cards—you'll win the game."

There's so much to remember, like royal flushes and full houses—names for the combinations of the cards.

Poker has a weird language. "Fold" means to quit, and "bluffing" is when you pretend you have better cards than you do. "Double barrel" betting and bluffing can throw your opponent's game off.

Opa is saying, "It's rare that a person has all the cards they need the first time around. Poker is a game of chance, just like life."

I divide the poker chips so that we each get fifty. We use them to make bets. Plus they're fun to stack.

Ginger carries a worry stone. Lots of things stress her out, like spiders, and mayonnaise, and whether she's going to get into a good dental school, like her mom did. Ginger claims that if you rub a worry stone ten times, things get better. I guess if it helps, then it's working, even if it's just made up.

I slip a couple of poker chips into my pocket for good luck. It can't hurt, right?

"Don't show any emotion." Opa holds his cards with one hand. I hold mine with two. "Don't ever let your opponents see your cards. Keep your eyes and ears open," Opa warns. "Players who talk the loudest are usually making up for their weak cards."

I learn when to throw down cards to get new ones, but I keep forgetting what cards you need to win.

"Wait!" I tell Opa.

When I return with my *Guest Check* pad notes, my grandfather is asleep. I retreat to my room and practice making a poker face in the mirror. That's when your expression goes blank so the other players can't guess what you're thinking or feeling. I wonder if anyone can tell that I'm homesick.

Chapter 15

We've been here three weeks and I've hardly gotten to talk to Ginger. The only phone my grandparents have is in the kitchen. Opa loves to include himself in the conversation. The other day he yelled, "Tell her I once had a spider bite that was so big it looked like I had a second head on my leg!"

Ginger's started hanging out with Maya and Andi. They're both super nice, but what if the three of them become best friends and Ginger forgets about me?

I'm at the train depot reading a book from Mom's shelf, *Blubber* by Judy Blume. Lazy Dog is napping in the shade. He raises his head when we hear whistling.

Logan is by the wishing well when a little kid with a fishing pole and a bucket walks up. "Hey, Finn!" he says. I hide behind my book. I'm not sure where we stand, especially since I was sort of mean to him the last time we saw each other. "How'd the worm test go?"

"Great!" Finn holds up his catch. Some are still wiggling.

"Thanks," Logan says. "I'll have more for you in a couple days."

Finn heads back into town, and Lazy Dog follows, but Logan is lingering.

"Hi, Logan," I finally say, putting the book down. "Worm test?"

He nods. "Not to brag, but my family owns the bait store. We have the best worms. I never charge Finn because . . . just because."

I look at Logan differently. I still feel bad for snapping at him at Ben Franklin.

"Well, I'm gonna go now," he says.

I'm half hoping he doesn't hear when I ask, "Would you like to hang out for a while?"

Instantly, Logan circles back. "Yes, yes, I would. THANK YOU!"

It's embarrassing how happy he looks, but I can't help smiling, too.

Chapter 16

I'm getting pretty good at poker.

"When you're playing, you need to know who you're dealing with." Opa sets his glass down. "Like life, a poker game never starts at the beginning. It's started before the player takes their seat at the table."

I refill his glass and pour myself one. We have lemon trees back home, but here lemonade comes from a powder. Opa continues. "Your opponents will give clues about their cards. It's called a tell, because a subtle change in how they act can tell you what they're thinking.

"For example, I asked you if you liked Last Chance, and you hesitated before saying, 'It's great!' That told me you were thinking about what to say. Plus, your voice was louder than normal, as if you were trying to convince yourself of something."

Opa pulls a handkerchief out of his sleeve, like a magician, and coughs into it. I hand him some fortune cookies.

"'Today will soon be tomorrow,'" Opa reads before tossing the little white slip of paper. "Good cookie. Dumb fortune."

I nod, but I'm busy thinking about tells. The other day, Oma practically said the same thing about Golden Palace diners: "The customers read the menu, and I read them. I can tell who's cheap and who's willing to pay for a feast."

I've watched Last Chance's town leader, Mayor Whitlock, argue that a half order of fried rice should be half the price. He doesn't understand that it takes the same amount of effort to cook half a dish as it does to cook a whole one.

Lady Macbeth always gets the most expensive items on the menu and leaves the leftovers. Men like to fight over who pays the check, and women are more likely to split the bill.

How a person eats tells a lot about them, too. Before she takes a bite, Oma waits, watching others' reactions to her food. Mom rearranges her plate so everything looks perfect. And Opa moves his food around so it looks like he's eating a lot, when really he's not.

"Opa, will you tell me more about Lucky?"

He pushes away his plate and nods. "Okay then, where were we? Ah, yes. Lucky had just heard of a place where there was a mountain made of gold. . . ."

Gold Mountain

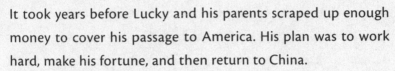

1869

It took years before Lucky and his parents scraped up enough money to cover his passage to America. His plan was to work hard, make his fortune, and then return to China.

The Pacific Mail Steamship Company's routes included Hong Kong, Shanghai, and San Francisco. The line was an official carrier of US government mail, but it also transported other cargo—Chinese immigrants. The ship was crowded with others who shared Lucky's dream, including Li Wei, another boy from his village. Conditions were harsh. Many people died, and their bodies were buried at sea. After almost fifty days and nights, Lucky's ship docked at the Gold Mountain—San Francisco, where just years earlier, men grew rich mining gold.

"At last!" Lucky cried to his friend. The two peasant boys marveled at the buildings that stood four stories tall and the cobblestone streets crowded with horse-drawn carriages. They laughed when they saw that the white men and women didn't have horns or fangs, as villagers had warned they would.

In the 1860s, Lucky was barely sixteen years old. The California gold rush was over, but most of the Chinese who had come to work in the gold mines remained. Even if they wanted to return home, they couldn't afford it. Their wages were lower than anyone else's for the same jobs. They had no rights in America, and because they looked different from the white people, they were treated with suspicion.

At least there was plenty of work. The Central Pacific Railroad, the western rail route of the first transcontinental railroad, needed laborers, and the Chinese were known to be hard workers who were willing to risk their lives to get the job done.

To lay down the railroad tracks, solid granite mountains had to be cleared, and the work was often deadly. One of the most dangerous tasks was when a "Chinaman" was attached to a rope and lowered down the side of a cliff. He'd hammer into the granite and insert a lit stick of dynamite; then it was up to the others to frantically pull him back up to safety before the explosion. As many as twenty thousand Chinese immigrants worked on the railroads. Tragically, hundreds lost their lives doing dangerous work.

Still, Lucky and Li Wei were relieved to have railroad jobs. It was better than starving in China.

Chapter 17

Mom and Oma are always arguing about little things, like the way my mother stacks the menus or that my grandmother saves piles of unread magazines. No one talks about the time my grandparents came to the TV commercial set and left without even speaking to my mother.

The strain between them is as thick as jook, the Chinese rice porridge Opa has for breakfast. He sprinkles it with green onions and bits of salted fish. I like it, too. Only, I add lots of soy sauce when Oma isn't looking. "Like perfume," I heard her tell Daisy, "soy sauce should be used sparingly."

Daisy's becoming an expert at deep-frying cream cheese wontons, something I am certain my ancestors never ate. At the end of her shift, Daisy collects food scraps for her compost bin behind the restaurant. Recently, she talked Oma into recycling, explaining, "Ninety-four percent of the United States population has access to a recycling program. That puts Last Chance in the bottom six percent. But it doesn't mean that the Golden Palace can't recycle on our own."

I think she just wore Oma down. Daisy kept blinking because she was so nervous. That's her tell.

When my grandmother finally said "Fine. But you're in charge of recycling. I don't have time to sort," Daisy was so happy that for the rest of the afternoon she sang Disney songs until Oma made her stop.

It's brave of Daisy to speak up for what she believes in, even though it was scary for her. I could tell that Oma thought so, too. I caught her sneaking extra money into Daisy's tip jar when she wasn't looking.

Chapter 18

Logan's just left the Golden Palace. We've hung out four times now. He loves being in the kitchen: "Where the magic happens!" Oma pretends he's in the way—but always manages to make too many cream cheese wontons when he's here. "You may as well eat them or they'll go to waste," she says.

Werner is sitting outside his restaurant in a green plastic chair. Logan told me that he and Opa used to be best friends, until something bad happened. Opa says we're not allowed to talk about Werner, though he did admit his food was great. Maybe if I bring home something from Werner's Wieners, Opa will get his appetite back.

Using my poker skills, I try to act cool. If my grandfather caught wind of what I was doing, I'd be in big trouble.

"You open for a deal?" Does Werner spot my tell when my voice wavers?

"You're Johnny and Lydia's granddaughter, aren't you?"

I nod. I suddenly recognize him from the Ben Franklin

soda fountain when I first arrived. He was the man in the orange sweater. "I'm Maizy Chen."

"What's the deal?" he asks as I follow him into the restaurant.

"Two of your best hot dogs for this." I hold up the lunch that was meant for Opa and me. Then I raise the stakes. In poker, that means increasing the bet. "Not only is there sizzling ginger beef, but there's also pork with a honey glaze." Who can resist that?

The smell of garlic and barbecue fills the room as I push the bag across the counter like it's a pile of poker chips. I'm all in—that's when you bet everything you have. Now it's Werner's turn. He can either "call," meaning he'll give me equal to what I've offered, or "fold," which is basically quitting. But who would quit when Golden Palace barbecue is on the table?

Werner looks curious. "Who's the bratwurst for?"

"For me . . . and a friend."

Technically that's true.

Werner eyes my bag as if sizing up the stakes. "Okay then." He lowers his voice even though I'm the only customer. "No one can know."

As the bratwursts sizzle and whistle on the grill, he asks casually, "How is your grandfather?"

"He's sick," I say.

Werner's back is to me. His shoulders tense. When he turns, Werner opens his mouth to speak, then closes it quickly as if changing his mind.

"Were you going to say something?"

Werner nods. "Yes, well. For the record, it's bratwurst or brat, not hot dogs."

Back home, Opa sniffs the air. Carlos! is in Frankenmuth, Michigan, eating buttered noodles and fried chicken. "What's that?"

I can tell by the way Opa leans forward that he already knows.

"Bratwurst. You want one? I have four." I only asked for two, but Werner put four in the bag.

Opa looks conflicted. "You didn't tell Werner these were for me, did you?"

I shake my head.

Opa eagerly unwraps the brats and hands me one.

"Three . . . two . . . one . . ." We both take a bite.

The homemade roll tastes like a salted pretzel on the outside, but is soft on the inside. The bratwurst is smothered in grilled onions, green peppers, and spicy mustard. Delighted, we burst out laughing.

Opa's eyes are closed as he chews. "No one can know."

It doesn't take us long to polish off the bratwursts. I've never seen Opa eat that much before!

"I taught Werner how to speak English," Opa brags.

"Really?"

"His family immigrated here when we were in grade school. They only knew German. Even though Werner and I didn't speak the same language, we became friends. For the longest time, I was the only one who understood him."

Sometimes Ginger and I are like that.

"He doesn't have an accent," I point out.

"That's because I'm a great teacher!" Opa looks pleased with himself. "Every day, I worked with him on his English. He taught me some German, too. That's how we became best friends."

"Werner is your best friend?" I thought they weren't speaking.

Carlos! takes a bite of spicy Cajun jambalaya and yells "Delish dish!" but Opa isn't paying attention. Instead, his face goes dark. "*Was* my best friend," he corrects himself. Opa looks at the empty brats wrappers, then at me. "I don't want to talk about him. Besides, wouldn't you rather hear about what happened next for Lucky?"

Life at Camp

1870

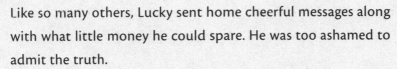

Like so many others, Lucky sent home cheerful messages along with what little money he could spare. He was too ashamed to admit the truth.

The Chinese weren't treated well. Besides having the most dangerous jobs and being paid less, they weren't even allowed to live with white people. Eventually, Lucky became the Chinese camp cook. He enjoyed preparing the dishes he'd watched his mother make. There was rice at every meal, and he could do wonders with fish or chicken, and fruits and vegetables. "It tastes like home," the men would say.

At night, while many gambled to pass the time, Lucky and Li Wei stayed up to talk. The stars looked the same here as they did in China. Though the boys were often homesick, at least they had each other.

One morning as Lucky was serving breakfast, the railroad foreman rode up to the Chinese camp on horseback. Wordlessly, he pointed to Li Wei.

A chill ran through Lucky. "You can't do it!" he begged his best friend after the foreman had left.

"Don't worry," Li Wei assured him. "I'll be fine."

Later, a loud boom shook the earth. Lucky fell to his knees. No one had to tell him what he already knew—Li Wei would not return.

Lucky kept his job as cook but knew he had to get away from the railroad. A few months later, a rumor circulated that there was an opening for a cook's assistant at the Philips Mansion in San Francisco. Everyone knew of Mr. Philips. He was one of the few white men who treated Chinese like humans instead of animals. His household staff, it was said, included Chinese servants. Lucky was determined to apply for the job.

Chapter 19

Sometimes late at night when Opa's asleep, I sneak outside, where the sound of Mom and Oma's arguing is re-
placed by crickets chirping. The stars are brighter here than
in Los Angeles. I always look for the Big Dipper first. Did
Lucky see it, too?

Opa says that Chinese immigrants helped build two
thousand miles of railroad. That's the distance from Los
Angeles to Last Chance. Does my mother know about any
of this? She's never mentioned it. I know Lucky wanted to
come to America. I wonder how my family ended up in
Minnesota. I can think of a hundred places I'd rather be—
like home.

In my room in California, I can look past the palm trees
and see the Hollywood sign nestled in the hills. Move the
letters around and you can make the words "old whooly,"
"howl dooly," and "hod woolly." There's always something to
do in Los Angeles.

I've been spending more time with Logan. He says there
are 11,842 lakes in Minnesota, including Lake Superior and

Last Chance's own Big Little Lake. People fish and picnic and sunbathe like they're at the beach back home. Sometimes we go to the lake, but I'm not a big fan of mosquitoes. Mostly we hang out around town and at the train depot.

At least Opa and I get to go to lots of exciting places when we watch Carlos! Mom is cautious, but optimistic, about Opa's health. Oma still insists that everything is just fine. There are topics she refuses to talk about, like what's the matter with Opa and the tension between her and my mother. Mom won't discuss that, either. They're more alike than they think.

Today Carlos! is in Iowa Falls, Iowa, waving around an ear of roasted corn wrapped in bacon. It's Bacon Week. Yesterday he had a bacon donut in Montclair, New Jersey.

"Everything is better with bacon!" Opa agrees with Carlos! "Maizy, Werner does a bacon brat that's in the 'delish dish' category." He gives me a sideways glance. "Not that I care."

I know what we're having for lunch today!

The bacon is frying as Werner asks me about Opa. Opa also asks me about Werner all the time. It's not just food I deliver. I also bring news to the two former friends about each other's lives.

"How's business at the Golden Palace?"

"Good," I lie. "Busy. How's business here?"

"Good," he says. "Busy."

I look around. There are no customers. "How come you're only open for lunch?"

"We used to be open for dinner, but when my wife passed four years ago—" Werner's eyes fill with tears. I look away to give him some privacy. "Onions," he mutters. "After Delores, it was too much for me to run the restaurant alone for both lunch and dinner."

I think about Oma.

"We have a daughter. She's a lawyer in Boston." He points to a framed photo on the wall. "Kaitlyn doesn't want to grill brats in a small town for a living, and I don't blame her."

I think about Mom.

"Running a restaurant is grueling work." He mops his forehead. Werner's Wieners doesn't have air-conditioning. "If Kaitlyn wanted to take over, I'd let her. But her mother and I worked hard here so that she could have a job she loved."

Could Oma be mad at Mom for her not wanting to take over the Golden Palace, or is it something else?

Carlos! was right. Everything does taste better with bacon! After we finish our bacon brats, Opa cracks open a fortune cookie. He hands his fortune to me.

The sun sets in the west.

Opa snorts. "A duck could write better words than these."

Suddenly I have an idea! I grab a bunch of fortune cookies and take off.

"Maizy, where are you going?"

"Quack, quack," I yell down the stairs.

Chapter 20

Earlier this morning at the restaurant, I took some of the old photos off the wall to examine them more closely. One almost crumbled in my hand.

I'm typing in Mom's room now, thinking about old memories and new ones. There's no delete key on this typewriter. I give up and reach for a pen. Getting the old fortunes out is easy. Putting a new one in is hard. After breaking three cookies, I manage to slip the fortune into the fourth.

Opa is still talking to Carlos! when I return. "Yes, bacon should be designated a national treasure!"

I hand the cookie to Opa. He looks curious and then laughs so hard I'm afraid he's going to hurt himself.

His fortune reads: You should tell your granddaughter a Lucky Story.

The Philips Mansion

1870

Lucky had never seen a palace before, but he was certain he was standing in front of one. The Philips Mansion was anchored on a hill overlooking the sparkling waters of San Francisco Bay. It was three stories tall, with stained glass windows that shone like jewels and marble stairs that led to a grand entrance.

The man who answered the door looked down at Lucky's tattered clothes and queue, the long braid only the Chinese wore. "We don't give handouts."

"Please, Mr. Philips." Lucky bowed his head. "I'm here for cooking job."

The man's laugh was cut short when a voice from inside the mansion called out, "Jenkins, is that an applicant?"

The kitchen was ten times as large as Lucky's hut back home. Black cast-iron stoves gave off the aroma of roasts and fresh-baked bread. Shelves were crammed with food, and bushels overflowing with fresh fruits and vegetables sat on the floor.

Jenkins held up his hand. He was wearing white gloves. "Wait here. Don't steal anything."

Lucky was too scared to move. He remained frozen until an elegant lady carrying a basket of roses walked in. Quickly he stepped aside to let her pass and was startled when she smiled at him. A woman wearing a long white apron rushed over to take the flowers. When the elegant lady left, the other woman nodded in her direction and said to Lucky, "That's Mrs. Philips, the mistress of the house."

Mrs. Birney was the cook. Her cheerful face put Lucky at ease as she asked about his cooking and listened to his stories about his mother's kitchen and the dishes he prepared for the railroad men. Unlike most white people, she didn't laugh at his Chinese accent or mock him when he couldn't find the right words.

Servants, both white and Chinese, moved in and out of the kitchen, sneaking peeks at Lucky. "I work hard and assist you and your kitchen in all ways," he promised.

"When can you start?" Mrs. Birney asked.

Chapter 21

After the last story, Opa told me, "Lucky loved working in the kitchen. Getting that job made him feel proud." I've been thinking about that for days.

Oma must really love the Golden Palace. She's always there. For me, helping out at the restaurant is fun, especially talking to Daisy. For my mother, it's stressful.

"You still use this wooden box?" Mom asks Oma. When she shakes it, you can hear the coins rattle among the dollar bills.

"There's nothing wrong with it." Oma sounds defensive.

"It's time you got a cash register," my mother tells her.

"We've been doing fine without one for decades," my grandmother snaps.

"One of the customers told me they were impressed by my English," I'm telling Ginger. Mom lets me borrow her phone now and then. "I think they meant it as a compliment, but it's sort of insulting."

"That kind of stuff happens to me a lot," Ginger says. "Only sometimes people are just being mean."

"Really? Like what?"

"Now and then a stranger will call me or my brother a 'dirty Mexican' or joke they're going to deport us."

I had no idea people were saying those horrible things. They don't say stuff like that at school, but there everyone knows Ginger.

Like me, she was born in Los Angeles. Ginger's a third-generation American. Her uncle is an officer in the Marines, and her aunt is a California state representative. But even if Ginger just immigrated last week, no one should be treated like that.

I'm meeting Logan outside Ben Franklin. We're going to have half-price hot fudge sundaes. He's running toward me and waves but doesn't stop. Logan's being chased by two boys. Separately, they're nobodies. Together, they're bullies.

The Mean Girls are coming out of Ben Franklin. They step aside when the boys run past. Riley, the beautiful one, isn't with them. Caroline smirks when she sees me. What did I ever do to her?

I think about the bullies who make fun of Ginger, and the ones in front of me now. One of the boys grabs Logan by the shirt. My heart starts beating fast—can they tell? I should do something, but I have no idea what—until I remember what

Opa told me: "Don't show any emotion. Don't ever let them see your cards."

"Stop!" I shout as loud as I can.

Immediately, they let go of Logan.

I had no idea I was that intimidating.

"Don't do it again," a man's voice says. "If this happened during school, you'd both be suspended. As it is, I'll be contacting your parents." Principal Holmes is standing behind me. His face softens as he helps Logan up. "You okay?"

"Sure!" Logan shakes off his embarrassment. "No hard feelings, right, guys?"

The bullies back away. After they turn the corner, I can hear laughing.

"See you around!" Logan calls after them.

I can't stand that Logan is being nice to the people who tried to hurt him.

Principal Holmes is looking at me with interest. Am I in trouble? "Maizy," he says, "it's admirable that you stood up for your friend. Your mother was that way, too."

Chapter 22

Mondays are the restaurant's slowest day of the week. That's when Oma teaches Daisy new recipes. Today it's General Tso's chicken. "This dish is more popular in America than in China, where few know about it," Oma tells her.

"It reminds me of Chicken McNuggets," Daisy muses while adding red chilies and garlic to hoisin sauce.

When my grandmother says, "Very smart of you to notice," Daisy stands taller.

Oma is adding salt and pepper to the cornstarch. "Some say that when McDonald's couldn't buy the recipe from the original chef, they created their own version and called them McNuggets."

Really? Wow! "Is that true, Oma?"

Instead of answering, she arches an eyebrow. Oma would be good at poker.

If you're willing to travel eighteen miles, there's a McDonald's in the next town. Mom says she and Principal

Holmes used to sneak away to get Big Macs when they were in high school.

"Growing up, all I wanted was pizza and hamburgers," Mom once told me. "It was bad enough that no kid looked like me—but no one ate like our family, either. It was Chinese food three times a day. To me, McDonald's was a treat."

"Is that why you never make Chinese food?"

"I've had enough Chinese food for a lifetime," she assured me.

Logan says all the cool kids hang out at McDonald's. Oma says that if I even think about going there, she'll disown me. Good thing she can't read minds.

Mayor Whitlock is passing out copies of *Minnesota Dontcha Know*. Instead of thanking him, Lady Macbeth says, "I remember when these used to be weekly."

"I write for the magazine," Mayor Whitlock tells a woman sitting at the table next to him.

"I read you every month!" she exclaims.

Mayor Whitlock acts like it's no big deal, but I can tell that he's pleased. "I also own Whitlock and Associates," he adds.

What he doesn't say is that it's just him. Logan told me there aren't really any associates, and Mayor Whitlock's public relations company's main client is the town of Last Chance.

There's a big commotion at table eleven. A noisy family

that loves the Monday Kids Eat Free special are at the big table. The dad never leaves a tip, so the mom always sneaks back to put a few dollars on the table. "You can tell a lot about a person by how much they tip," my grandmother told me.

Principal Holmes is here again, too. His T-shirt has a dinosaur reading a book on it. Does he come here for the food or to see my mother? Mom usually takes a long break to talk to him, but she's at home with Opa right now. She never takes a restaurant break just to hang out with me.

"Do you eat every meal at the Golden Palace?" I ask Principal Holmes.

"When I'm in town, pretty much. Though Werner serves up great bratwurst. You been there?"

"Kind of," I answer. "What do you mean, when you're in town?"

"I live in Minneapolis, a couple hours away." He pours himself more tea. "I have an apartment in Last Chance for when school's in session."

"But it's summer and there's no school."

Principal Holmes swirls the tea in his cup to cool it down. "I'm still here three or four days a week applying for grants for new computers for the library, more books . . ."

Computers? Library? Books?

He catches himself. "Boring!"

"Could I use the school computers and maybe check out some books?" I remind him, "The town library got flooded."

Principal Holmes strokes his chin. That's his tell. "Technically, Last Chance students aren't allowed on campus when school isn't in session."

"Technically, I'm not a Last Chance student," I point out.

Principal Holmes grins like in his prom picture.

"If it's okay with your mom, it's okay with me."

He leaves a six-dollar tip for a nine-dollar meal. Maybe he's not that bad after all, even though I'm not sure what's going on with him and my mom.

Chapter 23

A few days later someone knocks on the door. "Who is it?" Opa yells from the living room.

There's a long silence before a voice says, "It's me."

Opa's face sours. "Bolt the door, Maizy!"

I let Werner in. He looks uncomfortable.

"Why is he here?" Opa mutters.

I just shrug. I don't mention that I invited him.

Werner and Opa have their arms crossed and their backs to each other. Opa claims Mom and Oma are stubborn. Well, what about Werner and him?

Since the two aren't speaking, they use the television to carry the conversation. Luckily, Carlos! has enough to say for three people. Right now he's in Eagle Rock, California, dipping his pita into hummus and garlic sauce at King Kabob, a tiny Armenian restaurant with only three tables.

Opa and I love to yell "Delish dish!" along with Carlos! Logan has started watching with us, and the other day he shouted so loud that a neighbor called to see if everything was all right.

Right now the only person who's talking is Carlos! I look from Opa to Werner and back. Both have their mouths clamped shut. Adults are weird when they're mad at each other. They use silence as weapons.

It's late. The Golden Palace is closed, and Werner is long gone. Opa is surfing through the TV channels. I'm sitting on the floor, weaving ribbons through the spikes of his wheelchair. Eva gave me a bunch of them. Mom says colors can affect the way people feel about food and put them in a good mood. Maybe these colorful ribbons will cheer Opa up.

My grandfather stops on a food commercial. "Look! Fake milk!"

When Mom nods, he grins like a kid in school getting the answer right.

Oma is quick to point out, "See! Sharp as a tack. There's nothing wrong with him. He could see that immediately."

Opa jokes, "Old lady, admit it. You are going to be so sad when I die!"

"Old man, stop that talk!" she shoots back. "You're not going anywhere anytime soon! I forbid it."

They're always arguing like that. Is this love?

On Saturday Mom went to Saint Paul with Principal Holmes. They were picking up a used cash register and didn't come back until nearly dinnertime. When I asked why she was sunburned, Mom said they rented kayaks and paddled down the Mississippi River. Why wasn't I invited? Something is definitely going on between those two.

The laundry is warm from the dryer and smells like flowers. My mother used to go out with a man who always brought her roses. She was really impressed until she found out he was stealing them from our neighbor's yard.

"Have you ever been in love?" I ask.

Mom hesitates. "I've been in love, but it's never seemed to last."

She motions for me to sit next to her on the bed, then flings a sheet in the air so that it lands on us, making a tent. We haven't done this for a long time.

"Do you ever wish you got married?" Not that I ever want her to. I like that it's just the two of us, though having a sister could be kind of cool.

"Not getting married has saved me from getting a divorce." Mom laughs, trying to make this into a joke. "The only people who ever wanted me to get married are your grandparents. They're old-fashioned like that. But I was determined to have a baby, married or not."

"Who was my father?"

I know this story by heart but like to hear Mom tell it.

"He was a donor and going to law school. I know that he's Chinese, and is athletic. When you're eighteen, if you're curious, you can find out more about him. In the meantime, you're stuck with just me."

I hug my mother. I love being stuck with her and wouldn't know how to share her with anyone else.

"Is that why we never visited Last Chance before? Because Oma and Opa were mad at you for having me and not being married?"

"Maizy, honey, they were never mad at you. They love you. It's me they have a problem with. I keep disappointing them."

Now that I've spent time with my grandparents, I know how much they love me. Opa telling me Lucky Stories and teaching me poker. Oma always nudging food at me. "They love you, too," I want to tell Mom. But she's probably too busy arguing with Oma to see it.

When I come out from under the tent, I see a shadow scurry past the doorway.

Chapter 24

Mom is the only one who uses the cash register. It's been over a week and Oma still refuses to go near it, like it's a pair of smelly sneakers. I am going to make more special fortune cookies like I made for Opa for the two of them.

I've gotten better at it. So the cookies won't break, I microwave them under a damp paper towel for a few seconds. When they're soft, I can unfold them and switch out the slips of paper. Then I quickly refold them before they harden and wrap them back up. That's the easy part. Coming up with the fortunes is harder.

I'm about to start typing when I hear yelling.

Opa?!

He's standing inches away from the television. On the news, there are protests against refugees and immigrants. A politician is saying that immigrants should "go home" because the US is too full. When Mom and I drove here from California, it didn't look that crowded to me.

The scene reminds me of the name-calling and insults

Ginger gets, only on TV, hundreds of people are doing this all at once and waving signs and banners. I guide my grandfather back to his wheelchair. Though he isn't that heavy, I can feel the weight of Opa's anger.

"You'd think things would have changed by now," he says, sinking into his wheelchair. "But there's still lots of work to be done."

I remember how Lucky was treated. On the news, a reporter is saying, "In America, up to seventy-five percent of the farmworkers are immigrants who pay taxes. . . ."

"Lots of time, people don't think about the consequences of their actions," Opa says wearily. "When they put down others, it makes them feel better about themselves."

The Mean Girls laughed at me because they could. Did it make them feel better knowing that I felt bad?

"Can you tell me another Lucky Story?" I turn off the television.

Opa nods slowly. "Yes, there are things you should know."

"Chinaman"

1875

Working in the mansion seemed like a luxury. Lucky had his own room and Tuesdays off. For the next five years, he worked alongside Mrs. Birney, the cook. At first, he washed and prepped the vegetables. Later, Lucky was put in charge of soups, salads, and small dishes. Finally, Mrs. Birney had Lucky creating entire meals.

"When I retire, they won't have to look far to replace me," she said. Lucky didn't understand. "You." She pointed at him. "You should run the kitchen!"

Lucky's heart soared, but his happiness was cut short when Jenkins muttered, "He's just a dirty Chinaman."

In time, Lucky did become the head cook. He made enough to send money back to China and to save some, too. Mrs. Philips raved over his meals, whether it was a simple garlic roasted chicken for two or a fancy seven-course dinner for two dozen.

Mr. Philips was impressed by Lucky's punctuality. Before the start of every meal, he'd check his gold pocket watch and declare, "On time, again!"

Lucky felt safe inside the Philips Mansion. But outside was another story.

Gangs of white troublemakers roamed the streets. Lucky knew he was a target. They found it especially fun to cut off and collect the queues the Chinese men wore. No one ever got arrested for this. The Chinese weren't considered worth it.

Even though he had a kitchen assistant by now, Lucky preferred to select the fresh produce, meats, fish, and poultry himself. He was friends with all the suppliers in Chinatown, where he did most of his shopping, and they saved the best for him. Lucky would place a long pole over his shoulders with a bucket on each end to carry things, like they did in China.

One foggy morning, the buckets were heavy with vegetables, baking goods, and seafood. "You, Chinaman, STOP!" Lucky heard.

He froze.

"What's that on your shoulders?"

It was a police officer who had a reputation for being more crooked than the criminals.

"Groceries, sir. For the Philipses."

"Well, you're breaking the law!" The officer gave a toothy grin to the white men who gathered like wolves circling their prey.

Lucky tensed. He knew what was going to happen next. Someone knocked his baskets to the ground. The mob began to attack. Instead of stopping them, the policeman looked bored.

"The Sidewalk Ordinance bans Chinese from carrying laundry or groceries on a pole," he recited.

"I'm . . . just trying . . . to do . . . my job," Lucky sputtered between blows.

Above the taunts, the police officer shouted, "That stupid braid of yours is against the law, too!"

"Stop, please!" Lucky pleaded as his queue was chopped off, then held up like a trophy.

Lucky managed to stagger home, bloodied and bruised. When Lucky's assistant saw him, he was horrified. Despite Lucky's protests, he told the head housekeeper, who informed Mrs. Philips.

"We'll arrange for Jenkins to get whatever you need from now on," she insisted.

"I'll take care of him," the butler promised.

When the two were alone, Jenkins's smile slid off his face. "I don't work for you, and I don't take orders from coolies."

Chapter 25

Yesterday I asked Opa about Jenkins. "I don't like him," I said. "He's so phony, acting all nice around Mr. and Mrs. Philips."

"The racists who act friendly are the most dangerous," Opa told me as he stretched out on the couch.

Opa naps a lot during the day, then has trouble sleeping at night. That means that my grandmother hasn't been getting a lot of sleep, either, since she stays up with him. But Oma never complains.

Werner is visiting Opa again. They act like two strangers in a dentist's waiting room. Still, this is a good time to go to the school library, since Principal Holmes is in town. On my way there, I spot Riley, the really pretty Mean Girl, heading toward me. I attempt an I'm-so-cool-and-you-can't-hurt-me look in case she makes fun of me.

A mosquito buzzes near my ear and I slap my face.

Riley looks startled. "Bug," I say.

She bites her lip. Is that the natural color or is she wearing lipstick? I wear ChapStick. I like the waxy taste.

Out of nowhere, Riley asks, "Have I done something to offend you? Every time I see you, you glare at me."

I do?

I find myself asking, "You make fun of me?"

When Riley shakes her head, her long blond curls bounce in slow motion like in a shampoo ad. "I don't make fun of people."

"Your friends do," I point out.

"I know this probably won't make you feel any better"— she sounds embarrassed—"but they're mean to everyone."

"Why?" I hate that I don't hate her right now.

"I think it makes them feel better?"

Better about what? "Maybe you can tell them to stop," I suggest.

Riley hesitates. "They might get mad at me."

Does this girl even know how beautiful she is? I wonder what it would be like to be blond and beautiful. Or just blond. Or just beautiful.

"They'll still want to hang out with you," I say. "And if they don't, you can hang out with me."

When Riley doesn't respond immediately, I feel totally stupid. Why would she want to hang out with me?

"Thanks, Maizy." Before she takes off, Riley adds, "You know, you can ask them to stop, too."

The library lights buzz as they flicker on. While Principal Holmes starts up the computer, I browse the shelves.

"Can I check this out?" I hold up *The Season of Styx Malone* by Kekla Magoon. Ginger said it was a great book.

Principal Holmes nods, then smiles when he sees me studying his shirt. Today's has *Beryllium, Nickel & Cerium* on it.

"What does it mean?" I ask.

He starts, "The chemical symbols for those are BE, NI, and CE. . . ."

"BE NICE!" I exclaim. Now I'm smiling, too.

"Maizy, check out all the books you want. They're here to be read. Just bring them back when you're done," Principal Holmes says on his way out.

There's a poster of Maya Angelou on the wall and Black boys on the cover of the book I'm holding. Other than my family, they're the only people of color I've seen in Last Chance.

Chapter 26

I give Werner an Opa report every other day when we swap lunches. On the days I don't stop by Werner's Wieners, he visits Opa.

"I know you must think we're boring old men," he's telling me. "But we were spitfires in our day, always getting into trouble."

This sounds interesting. "Like what?"

Werner lets me sit on a stool in the kitchen. He throws onions on the grill, then chuckles. "One year, your grandfather's grandfather—"

"Lucky?!"

"Yes, Lucky! Someone sent him a box of Chinese firecrackers. Those are the ones that make a lot of noise. We were just boys, younger than you, and we took some. We didn't have any matches, so your grandfather had the bright idea of using the gas flame from the Golden Palace stove to light them. And that's exactly what we did—at dinnertime with a dining room full of customers!

"When the firecrackers went off, everyone screamed and ducked under the tables."

Werner is laughing so hard that he's crying.

"Your grandfather and I got in so much trouble." He wipes his tears away. "But it was worth it."

Opa's hands tremble when I hand him the bag of brats. I want to bring up the fireworks story, but he still refuses to talk about Werner. When Ginger got her Labrador puppy last year, we watched Zoomie get bigger and stronger every day. This is the opposite. My grandfather is slowing down and tires easily.

We're eating our lunch when Carlos! says, "Let's talk about where some of our 'all-American' dishes really came from! Did you know that apple pie was brought over by the English, Swedish, and Dutch? Potato salad is from Germany, baked beans is a Native American dish, and ice cream is courtesy of the Tang dynasty in China!"

"Ice cream is from China!" Opa says proudly.

I take advantage of his good mood. "Another Lucky Story, please?"

"Let's start where we left off . . . ," Opa says.

Accused

1875

Despite their great wealth, Mr. and Mrs. Philips never put on airs. Mrs. Philips gave generously of her time and money to the Orphan Asylum, the Free Public Library, and Chinatown's Society for the Betterment of Women, and hired several of the household servants from there.

In China, education was only for the elite. In addition to teaching Lucky how to run a kitchen, Mrs. Birney, the cook, had taught him something even more valuable. She taught Lucky how to read and write. Instead of throwing out Mr. Philips's old newspapers, one of the housekeepers saved them for him.

To Lucky, this was like gold. Over the years, newspapers were a window on the world, good and bad. A woman named Susan B. Anthony cast a ballot in the presidential election and was arrested, since women weren't allowed to vote. Something called the telephone was invented. In Los Angeles, there was a mass murder and lynching of almost twenty Chinese. Though Lucky couldn't understand all the news, the political cartoons were quite clear—"The Chinese Must Go!"

Meanwhile, in the mansion, small things started to go missing, like Mrs. Philips's diamond earrings and Mr. Philips's beloved gold pocket watch. One day, while the Philipses were visiting family in Los Angeles, four policemen barged into the kitchen.

"That's him, right there!" the head policeman yelled.

Startled, Lucky was surrounded. He recognized the officer who had given him problems in the past. "What have I done?" he asked.

The officer opened his hand to reveal jewelry and a gold pocket watch. "We found these in your room. You know what happens to a Chinaman who steals?"

Lucky hadn't stolen anything, but he knew that didn't matter. Before the police officer could grab him, Lucky ran to his room. The money he kept hidden behind his bed was still there. Then he slipped out the side door. He had to get away, fast. At the dock, Lucky managed to board a boat that carried him across the bay. The last time he had been on the water, he was arriving from China. When Lucky finally made his way to the train station, he pushed cash across the counter. "How far can this take me?"

The ticket seller looked up with interest. A Chinaman with money? "You can go as far as you want," he said.

Even though he had worked on the railroad, Lucky had never been inside a train before. Slowly, it pulled away and then built up speed. Instead of looking out the window like the rest of the passengers, Lucky shut his eyes, remembering that Li Wei had perished while helping build the railroad tracks. His heart ached and he was frightened. Lucky didn't know where he was going, or what he was going to do. He just knew that it was either leave or get lynched.

Chapter 27

It's been five days. I know Opa likes to take his time with the Lucky Stories, but I can't wait for the next one. "Are you ever going to tell me what happened to Lucky? It's keeping me up at night worrying about him!"

Opa has a mischievous look on his face. "Maizy, you must be patient. Like a game of poker, eventually all the cards will be revealed."

Patience is not something I am good at.

Opa's silver hair glistens in the sunlight. The doctor gave him permission to go out a couple hours a day as long as it doesn't cause too much stress. To my grandfather, the only place worth going out for is the Golden Palace.

"Is this as fast as you can go?" Opa shouts as I push his wheelchair down Main Street. Today he is full of energy.

The colorful ribbons on his wheels whirl around, making it look like he's riding on giant pinwheels. Everyone who sees us smiles and greets Opa by name. Lazy Dog trots after us, wagging his tail. A couple of people applaud.

"I've always wanted a parade," Opa jokes as he waves back.

"Bud!" my grandfather greets his old friend. Once inside, Oma acts like she hasn't seen him in ages, when it's only been about twenty minutes. Daisy squeals and waves, and Mom says, "Welcome home, Dad."

For a moment, my grandfather looks like a young man. He reminds me of Lucky. I feel like I've gone back in time, until I hear someone yell, "C'mon, Maizy, the worms aren't going to wait forever!"

"What's the smell?" Logan holds his nose. There are two big empty buckets on the back of his bike.

"I may have overdone it with the bug spray," I confess.

When we near the lake, he draws an X in the dirt with a stick and we each lug a bucket of water over to it. Putting on a game show host voice, Logan announces, "It's worming time!"

I shake my head. "I can't do this."

"Why not?" Logan unzips his backpack. "We earn four cents per worm! There are about a thousand worms in a pound, so say we get half a pound—that's twenty dollars!"

"I don't care how much we make, it's disgusting!"

Logan's too busy squeezing liquid soap into the water to listen to me. He swirls it around with the stick, then dumps it on the ground.

"What are you doing?!"

Logan just stares at the mud. It's amazing what you can hear when you're still. Birds singing, leaves rustling . . . me screaming. Dozens of fat, slimy worms are wiggling out of the wet dirt, like the dead coming alive in the graveyard.

"Don't just stand there, Maizy," Logan says as he tosses them into a bucket. "Pick up the worms!"

Reluctantly, I attempt to pick up a worm with a stick. When that doesn't work, I reach for a second stick to use like chopsticks, only it's like big, fat noodles . . . that wiggle. To my shock, by the end of the morning, I'm gathering worms with my fingers just like Logan. Ginger isn't going to believe this. I'm not sure I do.

Chapter 28

My grandfather lets out a thundering belch. I do one, too. Opa claims that belching is a sign of a good meal. Mom claims it's a sign of bad manners, but she's not here right now. I skipped the chow mein at dinner, instead focusing on the glazed pork.

"Were you always good at belching?" I ask.

"The best!" Opa boasts. "When we were kids, me and Werner . . ."

He lets that hang in the air.

"Do you have any photos of the two of you when you were young?"

Opa pretends to bristle. "What do you mean? I'm young now!"

"What about all those old photos at the Golden Palace, the ones in the office?" I hand Opa a fortune cookie. "Who are all those people?"

"Paper sons." I'm about to ask what that means, when Opa reads his fortune. "'Not only are you handsome, you're a master storyteller.'"

He laughs. "You have a way with words, Maizy. Okay, I think we left off about a hundred and thirty years ago. I sometimes forget the details. At my age, the memory gets a little shaky. Anyway, your great-great-grandfather was forced to flee San Francisco. . . ."

The pictures will have to wait.

Jesse James Gang

1876

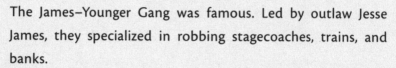

The James–Younger Gang was famous. Led by outlaw Jesse James, they specialized in robbing stagecoaches, trains, and banks.

On September 7, 1876, the gang was set to rob the First National Bank in Northfield, Minnesota. Their crew included a new man, Booth Francis, who was a cook in a town not too far away. Once at the bank, several men began shooting their guns into the air as a diversion while others stormed the building.

Inside, the bank cashier refused to open the vault. When Northfield citizens figured out what was happening, they began shooting back at the robbers. A battle broke out, leaving a by-stander, a banker, and two of the gang members dead as the gang retreated. In the next few weeks, the largest manhunt in the history of the United States managed to track down and catch or kill the outlaws. Except for Jesse and his brother Frank.

Meanwhile, an hour and a half away by horse, in the town of Last Chance, Minnesota, there was a problem of another sort.

"This food is awful!"

"I know, I know," the owner of the Golden Grille, the town's only restaurant, groaned. "But my cook's gone missing and it's just me in the kitchen!"

"Well, you'd better figure out something fast," the customer joked, "or the Golden Grille will be as dead as the James–Younger Gang!"

Three days later, a train pulled into the Last Chance Depot. Lucky peered out the window. The tiny town looked nothing like the big city he had left almost a year earlier. Lucky wasn't even sure where he was. He had changed trains so often to avoid detection, stopping sometimes for a few days or weeks, picking up work here and there.

"Sir," he asked the conductor. "Where are we?"

When a sheriff boarded the train, Lucky panicked. "This is Last Chance," said the conductor. Thinking he'd said "This is YOUR last chance," Lucky bolted.

The sight of a Chinese man sprinting down Main Street must have looked odd to the townsfolk, but Lucky didn't care. He had come so far and was still scared of getting caught, even though he hadn't done anything wrong. But when he got to the Golden Grille, Lucky stopped cold. A handwritten sign on the window read: *Cook wanted immediately.*

Chapter 29

I have so many questions! Could the Golden Grille cook have been one of the gang members? Opa keeps telling me to be patient. "You can't rush marinating char siu, and you can't rush a Lucky Story."

In the meantime, I've started looking up paper sons. When I pass the train depot, I imagine young Lucky stepping off the platform and looking down Main Street. There would have been a dirt road and horses instead of cars.

Back at home, Werner greets me. "He's such a stubborn old geezer," Werner says loudly as he leaves.

"Good riddance to that pest," my grandfather calls out before I close the door.

"Opa, was Lucky a paper son?" I ask.

My grandfather shakes his head. "Paper sons were young men from China who bought identity papers and pretended to be relatives of US citizens. So they were sons—but only on paper. Lucky was already living in America when they created laws to block Chinese from coming here. He wasn't one, but those photos on the office wall—most of those men were."

"Did he supply the identity papers?"

Opa yawns. Not talking to Werner wears him out. "No, nothing like that. Lucky didn't do anything that was considered illegal. What he did do, though, was help those in need. A place to stay, a meal, a job. And most of all, encouragement to any paper son who happened to find themselves in Last Chance."

"What happened to them?"

"I wish I knew, Maizy. We can talk more about paper sons, but there are other things you should know about Lucky first."

"Now?" I ask hopefully.

"It's nap time now," Opa answers with his eyes closed. "But I promise, you'll get more Lucky Stories."

Principal Holmes isn't at school on the weekends, so my paper sons research will have to wait. Opa's fishing vest has been hanging by the front door since I first arrived. "I'm going to pick up dinner. Can I wear this?" I ask, holding it up.

Opa yawns. "Sure, go ahead. It's not like I'm going to be reeling in those walleyes anytime soon."

I admire myself in the mirror. The vest is dark green with twelve pockets filled with cookies, binoculars, bug spray, and a couple of good luck poker chips.

Bud the Bear greets me at the Golden Palace. What I first thought was a menacing growl, I now see is a smile, probably from all those secrets he's keeping. Sometimes Logan and I hang out near him just to eavesdrop. We once heard a man confide to Bud that he was going to dress as a strawberry ice cream cone and propose to his girlfriend.

Opa loved when I told him that. He really misses the Golden Palace. The last time he was here, Opa tried to get out of his wheelchair and bumped into Daisy, who was carrying a plate of soy sauce chow mein. As she scrambled to clean up the mess, an awkward silence filled the room until he joked, "Poor girl didn't know what hit her!"

Everyone laughed, especially Opa. But I could see the shame on his face.

Right now, while Daisy is checking on the two huge rice cookers, Oma is in the office, muttering to herself again. The bills on the desk look like they've multiplied.

I look at the photos on the wall. I know who you are now. Hello, paper sons.

In most of the older pictures, no one is smiling. Later, there are some fun ones, including the skinny young man straining to hold a big bag of rice over his head. I notice faded cards and envelopes on the wall, too.

"The paper sons—do they have names?" I ask Oma.

"Everyone has a name," she answers.

"Whatever happened to them?"

Oma puts down her pen. "Why do you want to know?"

"When were they here? Wasn't it illegal?"

"Not everything illegal is wrong." Oma's keeping an eye on Daisy, who's lined up the carrots according to size. "I don't know the details about the paper sons who came through Last Chance. People didn't want others to know their business. It could be used against you. You never knew who you could trust."

"Do you know what happened to any of them?"

Oma shakes her head. "I wish I did, but most were from before I came to Last Chance. We lost track of so many over the years. It would be nice to know what became of everyone. I can only hope they went on to have happy lives."

The more I look, the more I see. Some of the men aren't much older than boys. Lucky was sixteen when he came to America. That's only five years older than me. I can't even walk into a room of strangers without feeling weird. Imagine entering an entire country of strangers. Behind all those serious faces in the photos, I can now see fear—but when I look closer, I also see determination, hope, and courage. It takes a brave person to cross an ocean for an uncertain future.

Oma guides me out of the office. "Paper sons. Real sons. Relatives. Visitors. They're all family. Whether for one meal, three days of a warm bed, or three months of work, it's an honor to help someone."

"How is it an honor?"

"When you're in a position to help, that means you're in a good place in your own life." Oma continues, "The train stopped coming through Last Chance a long time ago, and so did the paper sons. Maizy, our family didn't harbor criminals. We gave people food and jobs. There's no crime in that."

I think about the news Opa watches with people protesting against refugees and immigrants of color. Just last night there were reports about increased crime against Asian Americans. It's scary, what's on the news. But those things are happening in big cities, not small towns like Last Chance.

"Oma, how come you never talk about your family? Opa talks about his all the time."

"Mr. Motormouth talks enough for both of us." Just the thought of him makes her smile. Is that what love is? "Now, that's enough questions. Go take dinner to Opa! Shoo!"

Chapter 30

Summer is almost halfway over already. Opa's health is like a seesaw. Up and down. Some days he's alert and loves to talk, eat, and beat me at poker. Other days, he just sits and stares at the TV, even when Carlos! is on. It's those times that scare me.

I've been reading the *Minnesota Dontcha Know*s that Mayor Whitlock leaves in the lobby. He writes about lots of fun stuff, like twin cows who are best friends, and people who sail across the lakes in bathtubs. A short article titled "Searching for the Chinese in Minnesota" catches my attention. It's about a graduate student named Emmy Tsai who's doing research for her thesis.

I wonder if Emmy knows about the Golden Palace. Suddenly I have an idea! Oma and Opa try to act happy, but I can tell when they're pretending. If I can track down a paper sons family or two, that will cheer them up! Maybe Emmy can help?

I sneak some faded photos and papers into the fishing vest so I can make copies at the school library. On the back of a photo is an address in New Jersey. I study the young man in the picture. He has a buzz cut and is wearing a suit that's too small. His face is serious. In light brown ink, I can make out his name in curlicue handwriting at the bottom of the photo.

"Eddie Fong, whatever happened to you?" I ask out loud.

I know my odds are slim that his family still lives at that address, but I'm going to try writing to them. "You never know what cards will turn up," Opa likes to tell me.

When I get home, Opa and Werner are glaring at each other. While the two ex–best friends are busy not talking, I head upstairs and start typing. I make a lot of mistakes, since there's no delete key.

Finally, I have two fortunes I'm pleased with.

Good friends are friends for life.

Talk is overrated.
True friendships are not.

I swap out the fortunes and give a cookie each to Opa and Werner.

Chapter 31

The days are starting to breeze by. Daisy's now working full-time at the Golden Palace. This means that Mom and Oma can take turns spending more time with Opa, and I can hang out with Logan or help out at the restaurant.

I love talking to Daisy. "One of the highest points in Ohio is called Mount Rumpke. It's a mountain made of trash!" she tells me. When I look surprised, Daisy nods. "I knew you'd want to know."

There's a new sound in the kitchen to go along with the sizzling and bubbling and Daisy talking to herself. It's the clicking of the typewriter keys. I've decided that what the Golden Palace needs is custom fortune cookies. Ever since Oma gave me Wite-Out to paint over mistakes, typing's been easier. Our customers love my fortunes and have started asking for the special cookies.

"One per guest, per meal," Oma tells them. "Come back to the Golden Palace and you'll get another one."

For when I'm not around, I've written a bunch, like

You must be smart if you just had a meal at the Golden Palace! But when I'm at the restaurant, I watch the diners as if we were sitting around the poker table. Then I write their fortunes. . . .

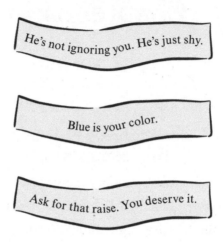

He's not ignoring you. He's just shy.

Blue is your color.

Ask for that raise. You deserve it.

It's Saturday night. A teenager named Erik Fisk is here with a date. They're at a table near Lady Macbeth. When he first walked in, I may have swooned slightly. He's so cute! I've seen him around town. Logan says Erik is the most popular boy in high school and acts like he rules the school.

So far, Erik has let me know that the tea is too cold, the soup is too hot, and the service is too slow. Erik snaps his fingers in the air to get my attention. Suddenly he doesn't look so cute anymore.

"There are supposed to be seven shrimp in this dish, but today there were only five."

He's really loud, like he wants everyone to look at him.

I remember Opa saying, "Players who talk the loudest are usually making up for their weak cards."

I'll bet Erik's the sort of person who bluffs all the time.

"I'm so sorry." I offer to bring him two more shrimp.

He tells his date, "You have to be careful with these people or they'll try to cheat you."

His date looks down at her lap. Nosy Lady Macbeth is watching.

Erik says to me, "I'll let it go this time."

"Thank you," I tell him. "And I'll let it go, too. Because I just counted seven shrimp tails on your plate."

Erik is still burning red when I bring fortune cookies and the bill.

His date reads her fortune and can't hold in her laugh.

"What's so funny?" Erik pays in cash and leaves a twenty-seven-cent tip.

"Nothing," she says.

Her fortune reads: You can do better than him.

When they leave, Erik glares so hard at me that I shiver. I distract myself by writing more fortunes.

Daisy's dream is for Last Chance to have a recycling program "with trucks that pick up, instead of me having to take everything to the recycling center." When she counts her tips tonight, she'll find a cookie by her tip jar with a fortune that reads: Smart people go green with recycling!

In poker, "the power of suggestion can unconsciously change behavior," Opa told me. "For example, if you nod when you get your cards, it signals that you have a good hand—whether you do or not. It guides how the other players think."

My fortunes are kind of like that. The power of suggestion, only in a cookie.

Chapter 32

It's an even day, so that means bratwurst. Even though Mom and Oma know that Opa isn't eating as much, they still make sure to pack full meals. That means Werner gets lots of food when we swap lunches.

"When Lucky was the cook, did he want to run the restaurant?" I ask Opa as I set the brat bag down. I'm not sure what I want to do when I grow up. Be a writer, maybe? "Was that his dream?"

"Sometimes people don't know their dreams until they're in it. Other times, their dreams escape them because they're too busy being busy. But for Lucky, fate, food, and good fortune presented themselves." Opa pauses to sniff the air, then continues, "Still, it was hard for Lucky. There were death threats, robberies, immigration officials, picky eaters— but you don't want to hear about all that, do you?"

"Opa, you know I do!" I hold up the bag from Werner's. "A story for brats and sauerkraut," I offer.

Golden Grille

1876

Not much usually happened in Last Chance, Minnesota, but overnight things got interesting. The Golden Grille, one of the few places to eat for miles around, had a new cook. Rumor was that he was a Chinaman . . . from California . . . and his food was delicious.

The grizzled old restaurant owner, nicknamed Happy, couldn't mask his enthusiasm. "Lucky, why are you always hiding in the kitchen? Come meet your fans!"

Even though the odds were slim of the San Francisco police bothering to track him down in Last Chance, Lucky worried about getting arrested for a crime he didn't commit. His heart grew heavy at the thought of Mr. and Mrs. Philips believing he had betrayed them. If this tiny town lived up to its name as Lucky's "last chance," he was determined to make the most of it.

It took months before he ventured into the dining area, and when he did, the room went silent. For most, Lucky was the first Asian person they had ever seen.

"What are y'all staring at?" Happy yelled. He pointed to the dishes. "That steak! Those buttermilk biscuits! The apple pie! This man made that delicious food you've been eating. Thank him!"

To Lucky, the stares and silence made him want to turn around and disappear back into the kitchen. But then the strangest thing happened. One gruff-looking man stood . . . and started clapping. Soon the whole room was cheering. Happy beamed like a proud parent watching Lucky go from table to table introducing himself.

"Lucky, your English is excellent!" one man said.

"His English may be excellent," another pointed out, "but his cooking is even better!"

For the next ten years, Lucky worked for Happy. Everyone knew that for a great meal, the Golden Grille never disappointed. Lucky had become one of the most popular citizens in Last Chance.

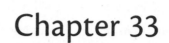

Chapter 33

On Sunday, when I come down the stairs, I can hear Mom and Oma arguing. This makes my stomach hurt. Opa is staring at the news and either can't hear them, is pretending not to hear them, or just doesn't care. There's no time for jook, so I grab a banana for breakfast.

Logan wants to worm again. There's a big demand for live bait in the summer from both locals and tourists who come to Last Chance for the fishing. As much as I hate worming, I can use the money.

Logan's on his bike and I'm walking alongside through town when he suddenly slams on the brakes.

"What?" I ask, annoyed. Also, why is there no trash can around here? Daisy says banana peels can take up to two years to decompose, so you shouldn't just toss them in someone's garden.

Speechless, Logan is pointing to the Golden Palace. I drop the banana peel on the sidewalk. The spot where Bud usually stands is empty. I run behind the building and call his name, just in case. Just in case what? It's not like a giant

wooden bear can get up and wander around. I'm not thinking straight.

"Who would take him?" Logan is pacing back and forth.

I spy Werner hauling boxes into his restaurant. Eva is wa-
tering the potted plants in front of Ben Franklin. Neither
seems to notice that Bud is missing. That's when I see it. A
note tucked into the door.

We have ur bear. If u want him back pay $1,000 yen
+ 12 egg rolls—or else GO HOME TO CHINA!!!

Mom is sprinting to keep up with Oma. Logan is guarding
the empty space where Bud once stood. A car slows as it
passes. I recognize the customer who always complains that
the food is too spicy and wants his money back—after he's
eaten the entire dish.

"It's true!" Oma is out of breath. "Bud is gone."

Mom and Oma stand shoulder to shoulder and read the
note together.

"Don't tell Opa," Oma whispers. "He loves that bear."

Just then bells ring and parishioners spill out of the
church down the block. Several stop by and ask, "Where's
Bud?"

"Missing," Mom says. She sounds uncertain.

Mayor Whitlock strolls over, holding a cup of coffee.
"Where's the bear, on vacation?"

The words tumble out of Logan's mouth: "Bud's been kidnapped. Criminals, I'm sure. They left a ransom note and it's rude."

Mayor Whitlock turns serious. "May I see it?"

We all await his verdict.

"This isn't just a prank," he says, handing it back to me for safekeeping. "This is a hate crime."

Chapter 34

Instead of worming, I head back with Mom and Oma. No one talks the whole way. When we get home, Opa's deep in conversation with Carlos! "Yes." He agrees. "Everything is better with butter!"

When Opa suggests a game of poker, I nod. Maybe that will help me get my mind off Bud. Only, before I even shuffle the cards, Opa has figured out my game.

"I can read a room, the same way I can read a table." He fixes his eyes on me. "Maizy, I can see that something's wrong. Oma went to the Golden Palace with her slippers on." I pretend I don't know what he's talking about, but Opa calls my bluff. "Tell me."

I take the ransom note out of the fishing vest and hand it over.

Opa studies it in silence, then faces the window. I can't read his face. "Bud is Last Chance's oldest citizen, and one of its most popular ones." Opa wheels around to face me. "Shall I tell you how he came to the Golden Palace?"

Budai the Bear

1886

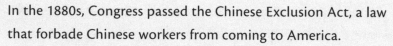

In the 1880s, Congress passed the Chinese Exclusion Act, a law that forbade Chinese workers from coming to America.

NO MORE CHINESE! the headlines shouted.

"What's the matter?" A grizzled face peered over the top of the newspaper Lucky was reading. Happy couldn't read very well, and his eyes weren't as good as they used to be, so he relied on his friend for the news.

"They don't want men like me here." Lucky's shoulders slumped. The two were having their usual early lunch before opening the restaurant. "They could ship me back or worse."

Lucky was now thirty-three years old. He had spent more of his life in America than in China. If you closed your eyes, he sounded like everyone else in Last Chance.

"Aw, you belong here as much as I do," Happy said. "I came from Germany, but we're both Americans!"

"You're white and look American," Lucky pointed out. "Plus, you're a business owner. It's the workers they're after."

Happy poured himself a drink, as he often did at any hour

of the day. "Friend, I'm too old to run the Golden Grille without you. Promise me you'll never leave."

That night, a wild idea woke Lucky up. It was a long shot, but he was so excited he couldn't go back to sleep.

The next morning, Happy and Lucky struck a deal. Ten years after he started as a cook, Lucky bought the Golden Grille, becoming one of the first Chinese businessmen in Minnesota. Happy was so thrilled that the day the restaurant officially changed hands, he gave the new owner a gift.

"Well, Lucky, don't just stand there. Say something!"

Lucky admired the huge black bear carved from wood. It stood outside the restaurant as if guarding it. "In China, when you see a statue of a monk named Budai, you rub his belly for good luck, happiness, and riches," he told Happy. "We may not have Budai the monk, but Budai the Bear's our own Chinese American good luck charm!"

With Happy as his enthusiastic taste tester, Lucky soon began adding Chinese dishes to the menu.

"What's this?" Sheriff Swain pointed to his plate. "Is it spaghetti? My brother lives in New York City and says spaghetti is the new big thing."

Lucky explained that these Chinese noodles were called lo mein, and it was his mother's recipe. When the sheriff, who was a picky eater, asked for another serving, Lucky knew he had a hit.

As the years went on, there were eventually more Chinese dishes on the menu than traditional American ones.

Lucky had a guarantee: if you didn't love the Chinese food, he'd replace it with an American meal for free. No one ever took him up on it.

One day a group of rowdy travelers sat themselves at the best table. "China food?" one complained, throwing down the menu. "What about steak and potatoes?"

"We serve that, too," Lucky explained.

"This is your place?" another said, shocked. "Since when do they let Chinks own a business?"

A third traveler laughed. "He's probably gonna serve us rats!"

Lucky had seen men like this before. It was best to get them fed and out of the Golden Grille as soon as possible. "The meal is on the house. Just tell me what you'd like."

"I'd like you to leave this country," the first man said. "And if you don't, we'd be happy to help you."

Chapter 35

We're both quiet for a while. Finally I say, "Opa, they threatened Lucky." I stop and whisper, "And they called him a Chink. Isn't that a really bad word?"

My grandfather nods. "Threats and worse happened a lot back then. And you're right. That word is one of the worst things you can call a Chinese person."

"Has anyone ever called you that?"

"Quite a few times, actually. Especially when I was younger, before the civil rights movement. But even after that, too. You can forget that there are prejudiced people out there and think things are good. Then one comes along, you're surprised all over again."

Opa is too exhausted to continue. I think Bud's disappearance affected him more than he's letting on. It's shaken all of us. "That bear has been part of the family for generations," Opa says after I bring him a cup of tea.

I wish I could make it better. But how? Carlos! is on the television digging into shrimp and grits in Mentone, Alabama. I know what I can do. It won't bring Bud back, but it would make Opa happy. It's a long shot, but like with poker, you can't win if you don't play.

Dear Carlos!,

My name is Maizy and I am almost twelve years old. My grandparents own the Golden Palace in Last Chance, Minnesota. The restaurant has been here for over a hundred years.

 Everyone says that the Golden Palace has the best Chinese food. There's one customer who loves everything so much, she always orders more than she can eat! If you could come do a show here, that would be great.

Sincerely,
Maizy Chen

P.S. My grandfather is your biggest fan. He's very sick, so if you can come soon, that would be great. Thank you.

Chapter 36

I reread the ransom note, looking for clues. It doesn't make sense. There's no signature or email or phone number. No one has tried to contact us. Yen is Japanese money, not Chinese. Plus, how can we "go home" to China if we've never even been there?

It's taken two days for the sheriff to show up. Apparently, missing bears are not a priority.

"So far, we have no suspects. It's probably just kids," he says.

"Does 'just kids' make it okay?" I ask.

The sheriff ignores me as he eats his lunch special. He leaves before the bill arrives.

Mayor Whitlock wants an interview for *Minnesota Dontcha Know.* "Bud the Bear is as close to a landmark as Last Chance has ever had," he says.

The next day at breakfast, Oma places bowls of jook on the table. "Business is bad enough already. Is this the kind of publicity we want for the Golden Palace?"

"We can't ignore what happened. People should know. I'll do the interview," Opa volunteers before a coughing fit sets in. He winks at me and I smile back. Opa's right. We can't let this go unnoticed.

"No, Dad," Mom cautions. "The doctor said for you not to get excited."

Oma and my mother exchange worried glances. No matter how much they argue, when it comes to Opa, they're always on the same side.

As the three of them talk, I recall Opa once telling me, "Maizy, if you want a big poker payoff, you can't be afraid to take risks. Get to know your comfort level, then push." I also remember Oma talking about helping others.

I clear my voice to get their attention. "I know who could do it," I say.

We're having lunch on a bench at the train depot. Logan's just finishing making another wish in the well. "The more wishes you make, the better your odds are that one will come true."

I hand him a container of cream cheese wontons. Oma added peanut butter to his, the way he likes it.

"Maizy, the interview will make you famous!"

I laugh. I'm not sure how many people actually read *Minnesota Dontcha Know*. "What if I say something dumb?"

"Mayor Whitlock can edit it out," Logan assures me.

"Gee, thanks." I'm getting pretty good at chopsticks. Opa

says when I can pick up a single grain of rice, he'll give me a present I'll never forget.

Before heading home, we stop at the school, where Principal Holmes lets us use the copy machine.

MISSING BEAR

Answers to "Bud"

Height: 7 feet

Last seen in front of Golden Palace on Main Street

REWARD FOR SAFE RETURN—one week of free meals

If you have information, please come to
the Golden Palace and ask for Maizy.

At home, I show Opa the flyer, explaining, "Logan and I put them up all over town."

He nods. "This isn't the first time something bad happened to Bud."

"Really? What else?"

Opa stretches his skinny arms. "That bear's no spring chicken, you know. We'll have to go back over a hundred years. . . ."

Troublemakers

1891

On the night the travelers showed up, long after the Golden Grille closed, Lucky heard pounding and yelling. Lucky opened the door and came face to face with the travelers. He could smell whiskey on their breath.

The three men dragged him into the street, laughing and yelling slurs. They threatened to lynch him. Fortunately, Lucky's time in San Francisco had taught him how to fight, and doing heavy work at the restaurant gave him muscles. Lucky managed to knock out one man, but there were still two more. He was about to throw another punch when he froze. A gun was pointed right at him.

Slowly, Lucky raised his hands. Had he traveled from China to America only to be killed by a drunk in Last Chance?

Just when he'd almost given up hope, Sheriff Swain arrived, backed by a posse that included Happy and several locals. "Leave that man alone!"

The man holding the gun was so drunk he could barely stand. "Aw, we was just cleaning up the town for you."

"Get out of Last Chance and don't ever come back," Sheriff Swain ordered.

"Who's gonna make me?" the man asked, shooting the gun into the air.

Lucky and the posse ducked for cover as the bullets flew.

Finally, when the man ran out of bullets, there was silence. But that was broken when Happy shouted, "Oh no, he's been—"

Chapter 37

"I think that's enough for today." Opa stretches his arms and yawns.

"No!" I cry. "You can't stop now. Was Lucky shot? Did he survive?"

Opa chuckles. "If he didn't survive, then you and I wouldn't be here today. Besides, it wasn't Lucky who took the bullets."

"Was it Sheriff Swain? Opa, tell me what happened!"

His eyes shine as he pretends to be annoyed. "Oh, all right, since you're being so pushy. . . ."

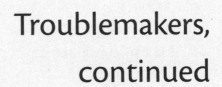

Troublemakers, continued

Bud the Bear had two bullets lodged in him, but he was still standing. With the troublemakers run out of town, Lucky returned to the Golden Grille, bolting the doors behind him.

The next morning, before sunrise, he awoke to the sound of glass shattering and the smell of smoke. Immediately, Lucky started tossing water onto the flames, but it was too much for one man.

"HELP! FIRE!" Lucky cried out.

The town was asleep, and as the flames rose, Lucky feared no one could hear him. Suddenly the church bells began ringing. Townsfolk spilled out of their homes, many still in nightclothes. Luckily, it had rained earlier in the week and the wells were full. A bucket brigade was created to throw water on the flames.

"I should've tossed them in jail when I had the chance," Sheriff Swain said.

"You'll be the one in trouble if you try to arrest white men for attacking a Chinaman," the mayor said, speaking the truth.

Though the damage was bad, the kitchen hadn't been

touched. For the next two weeks, Lucky worked nonstop repairing his restaurant. Friends pitched in, but on the day the Golden Grille was set to reopen, customers were greeted with a sign on the door: *Closed Until Further Notice.*

Lucky had gone missing.

Chapter 38

Even though the fires were over a hundred years ago, I walk around examining the Golden Palace walls. I don't care that Lady Macbeth is watching me. In a couple of places, I can see what looks like scorch marks. I search for Oma to ask her about them, but she and my mother are arguing about the cash register again. Opa got some medical test results back today. They weren't what my grandmother wanted to hear, but she never lets Opa know how worried she is. Instead, she takes her frustrations out on Mom.

Before I leave the Golden Palace, I type up fortunes for the customers. It feels good to brighten someone's day.

The woman who read a book during her meal gets one that says: Books + Chinese Food = Happiness.

It will grow back goes to a man whose wife accidentally cut off too much of his hair on one side.

The last two I type are for Oma and Mom. They say the same thing: Fighting is easy. Forgiving is hard.

On my walk through downtown, I study everyone I pass. Bud's kidnapper could be right in front of me. Most of the flyers are still up. On a couple of them, someone has drawn slit eyes on Bud. I throw those in the trash.

I'm so happy when I get to the school library and check my email. Emmy Tsai, the graduate student who was in *Minnesota Dontcha Know*, wrote back! She says she's heard of the Golden Palace and would love to know more. *Also, I'm in several research groups and would be happy to answer any questions I can.*

I reply and ask about Last Chance's paper sons. When I'm done, I browse the books. In the reference section, there are rows of yearbooks. I have to go way back, but I find the one from Mom's senior year. I know my mother loves to go running around the reservoir near our house in LA, but I didn't know she was on the track team. She's hardly ever talked about high school. I stop at a photo of Mom and Principal Holmes that's captioned: *The Odd Couple.*

My mother's senior quote is: *Goodbye, Last Chance. Hello, world!*

Principal Holmes's is: *What doesn't kill you makes you stronger.*

When I get to a photo of Mom eating in the cafeteria, the caption reads: *Don't mess with Dragon Lady's lunch!*

I slowly shut the yearbook and slip it back onto the shelf.

Chapter 39

I n the Whitlock & Associates Public Relations lobby there are stacks of brochures with headlines like *Your First Stop for Great Fishing—Last Chance!* Gold-framed covers of *Dontcha Know* line the walls. All feature articles that Mayor Whitlock has written, like "Prince, the One True King of Minneapolis."

I admire the silver statue of a woman holding a pen. "That's the J. Daniels Award, for excellence in journalism," Mayor Whitlock tells me. "I used to write about weightier things than who carved the best cow out of butter at the state fair. My goal is to get back to more substantial work and win it again one day."

I'd like to see a cow made from butter.

". . . this is the perfect story," Mayor Whitlock is saying. The wooden chair is uncomfortable. My feet don't reach the floor. I'm not sure what to do with my hands, so I sit on them. "There's the local angle of the beloved bear, the racial overtones—"

"But won't this article make Last Chance look bad?"

I'd think that as the mayor and public relations person, he wouldn't want that.

"Any publicity is good publicity," Mayor Whitlock assures me. "So tell me, Maizy, how do you feel about what's happened?"

"I feel terrible." How else would I feel? "If this is a prank, it's not funny."

Mayor Whitlock is writing down what I'm saying even though he's also recording. He points his pen at me. "Do you have any idea who might have done this?" I sneak a peek at his legal pad. His handwriting doesn't match the ransom note.

Some Golden Palace customers think it's hilarious to order in fake Chinese accents. It's possible the Mean Girls had something to do with it. But my number one suspect is Erik Fisk, who I embarrassed in front of his date. But I don't have proof.

"I really don't know for sure," I admit.

"What would you say to the person or persons who did this?"

"I'd say, 'Why did you take Bud? Why did you write that letter?'" I think about Lucky and Li Wei. "'My family's ancestors helped build America, so why do you try to tear us down?'"

"Good. That's good." He's drawn a maze on the paper. "You have a way with words."

I blush. I can't believe we've been talking for over an hour. "When will the article be out?"

Mayor Whitlock stops recording on his phone. "*Minnesota Dontcha Know* is a monthly magazine. This article won't run until August first, but I'm required to turn it in at least two weeks in advance. Once it's in, there can't be any changes. If you think of anything else, let me know soon."

He walks me to the door. "What's happened is newsworthy, but I'm sorry your family had to go through this, Maizy."

Chapter 40

O pa says that my bluffing skills are stellar, but I need to be more aggressive.

I shuffle the cards while Opa continues. "When you're up against multiple players, you need to know your position. That means the order people play."

Opa points to my *Guest Check* pad, where I'm taking notes. "Every hand of cards tells a story. Write that down."

This morning Opa ate most of his breakfast. Oma was really happy when this happened. Maybe he's getting better!

"It's best to go last," I recite as he cuts the deck, "so you can see what cards everyone else is playing."

"You got it!" Opa looks so proud.

Keeping track of the poker cards is kind of like keeping track of the suspects who might have kidnapped Bud. Everyone is in the game at first. But slowly, cards are tossed aside and others come into focus.

I throw down my cards—three eights and two kings. A full house!

Opa taps my cards. "Full houses are my favorite hand. Now, let's talk about how to set a trap."

"It sounds dangerous. . . ."

"Not if you do it right." He attempts to hide a yawn. "Setting a trap is when you pretend to have a weak hand of cards. You trick your opponents into a false sense of security and then pounce!"

I think about who might have taken Bud. Erik? I try to imagine Opa, Logan, and me pouncing on him.

"Opa, do you think we'll ever get Bud back?"

"Bud's a big bear," my grandfather reassures me. "He can't have gone far."

Later, I turn on the TV to keep Opa company while I pick up our lunch.

"Bears love salmon," he points out as Carlos! chews on smoked salmon jerky in Ketchikan, Alaska.

I walk downtown and go over the suspects in my mind. In poker, you don't just focus on the cards, or what's obvious, but take in all the other players—who they are, what they are doing, how they act. Opa says this is called reading the table. Only, instead, I'm reading the town.

I'm leaving Werner's when I spy the Mean Girls. The one named Caroline is talking to Erik. "Mom says you're in big trouble for staying out late again."

"Chill, sis. It's summer." He bumps into me, knocking my

bag of brats to the ground. Instead of helping me pick it up, he keeps going. "Oops."

Did he do that on purpose? I know he has issues with me—but are they big-enough-to-steal-a-bear kind of issues?

"I thought you people just ate rice," Caroline says while I scramble to pick up the food.

I try not to let this bug me when I remember what Riley said: "You can ask them to stop, too."

I stand and face her. "Why would you say something like that?"

She looks surprised. "Well, you're Chinese, right?"

"They eat other foods," the other Mean Girl chimes in with a laugh. "Like egg rolls."

"Why is that funny?"

The Mean Girls look confused.

"We gotta go," Caroline says, grabbing the other's arm.

"It was fun talking to you," I call out after them.

Now I'm the one who's laughing.

Chapter 41

One of the paper sons replied! Well, not the paper son himself, but his granddaughter. Her name is Lynn Fong, and she still lives in New Jersey with her husband and kids. Ms. Fong emailed that her grandfather Eddie had passed through Last Chance in the 1930s. That means he would have been helped by Opa's father, Philip, and maybe even met Lucky.

Emmy had told me that America's paper sons history is scattered across the country. *It's important to connect the dots,* she wrote. Now California, New Jersey, and Minnesota are linked.

I wrote back to Emmy, telling her about Lucky, and asked, *Can that happen again? Can groups of people be targeted just because of what they look like?* This has been bothering me ever since Opa started the Lucky Stories.

I hope I don't scare her away with all my questions.

———

It's dinnertime. Eva gave me a berry pie to bring to Opa.

"I'm glad Lucky changed the menu to Chinese food." I cut two generous slices. "But I'm worried. In the last story, he disappeared. I don't think I can go any longer without knowing what happened to him."

Opa takes a bite of pie and nods with appreciation. I see that familiar glint in his eyes. "Maizy, you want to know what happened? Well, let me tell you. . . ."

Return

1891

Happy was scared. "What if Lucky wandered off into the woods and accidentally drowned in the lake?" Others speculated that he went to work for a Chinese businessman who had opened a store in Saint Paul. A little girl thought she saw him board the train, but no one listened to her.

When Lucky returned to San Francisco, it was bigger, bolder. Chinatown now housed over twenty thousand residents crammed within twelve tight blocks. It was its own city, with its own shops, restaurants, and laws. On a couple of occasions, Lucky spotted Mrs. Philips going in and out of the Society for the Betterment of Women.

For the first week, Lucky stayed in Chinatown, building up courage for what he needed to do. It had been decades since he left China, and over fifteen years since he fled California. Here, surrounded by Chinese, no one stared at him. Still, Lucky wasn't sure where he belonged. He recalled his talks with Li Wei about returning to China a rich man and taking care of his parents. But they had passed away a long time ago. Lucky missed his mother and father. And he missed working for Mr. and Mrs.

Philips. They had trusted him enough to employ him and give him a chance.

Lucky drew a deep breath. If what he had to say didn't go well, he could face prison, or worse. A petite young Chinese woman answered the servants' door of the mansion. Not knowing if she spoke English, he said in Chinese, "My name is Lucky and I'm here to see Mr. Philips." The words sounded thick on his tongue. He hadn't spoken Chinese in years.

The young housekeeper tried to hide a smile as she motioned for him to wait in the kitchen. Not much had changed, although Lucky did admire the electric-powered lights.

Unlike his first visit, when he was dressed in his dusty railroad clothing, this time Lucky sported brand-new western clothes that were custom-tailored for him in Chinatown. His suit was dark gray, and he wore leather shoes and a black bowler hat. Several of the servants glanced at Lucky with curiosity. They weren't used to seeing one of their own in a white man's fancy business clothes.

"Lucky?!"

It was his former assistant. The two embraced, but before they could talk, a white butler who Lucky didn't recognize announced, "Mr. Chen, Mr. Philips will see you now."

Lucky's heart was racing. How would he be received? Would Mr. Philips call the police? Had he already?

Chapter 42

Oma is at home with Opa now. When I left, neither was speaking. But unlike with Opa and Werner, both looked delighted just to be in each other's company.

Was Lucky happy here in Last Chance? When I near the Golden Palace, I try to look at it the way Lucky would have the first time he got off the train. I'm not just walking into a building—it feels like I'm walking into a story.

In poker, chance and luck determine the cards you are dealt. Lucky didn't have much chance for success. So many things were working against him. "Yet the harder he worked, the luckier he got!" Opa insists.

Is that why Oma works so hard at the Golden Palace, and Mom is so successful at her job? If I could be lucky at something right now, it would be to bring Bud home. What are my chances of that happening?

Lazy Dog is sleeping where Bud used to stand. Daisy has started to leave a bowl of leftovers out for him every afternoon. Inside, Mom keeps trying to seat some customers while Lady Macbeth gives her a Minnesota goodbye. That's when you stand around talking for twenty minutes before leaving.

Daisy's counting her tips. "I did pretty well!"

"What will you spend it on?"

"You promise not to laugh?" Daisy asks. I nod. "I'm saving to go to school to get my master recycler/composter certificate."

I didn't even know that was a thing. "That's great!"

"Really? You think so?" Daisy's face is flushed. "My dad always told me I wasn't very smart. He wasn't a nice person. That's why I had to get away and ended up in Last Chance."

I hug Daisy and say, "I'm glad you're here."

She hugs me back tight.

Daisy's always rattling off recycling facts. Just yesterday she told me, "Over one million plastic bottles are used *per hour.*"

She's smarter than she thinks.

Chapter 43

Who stole Bud is still a mystery. It could have been a visitor, like those men who shot at Lucky and hit Bud instead. Or . . . it could be a local, like the Mean Girls or Erik. I'm at the school library looking up the townspeople to see if I can find any motives. It's kind of fun. Principal Holmes was once a member of a Minneapolis barbershop quartet. Eva's strawberry pie won a ribbon at the Minnesota State Fair. And from Mayor Whitlock's *Dontcha Know* article, I learn that a real cow weighs about a thousand pounds and a butter cow weighs six hundred.

I'm about to log off the computer when I get an email response from Emmy. I had told her about Bud's kidnapping and asked her a bunch of questions.

Hi, Maizy,

I can see why you find the laws surrounding Chinese immigration to America confusing.

During WWII, China and America were on the

same side. It would have been awkward if the US was banning Chinese immigrants, so in 1943 the Chinese Exclusion Act was repealed. But even then, only about a hundred Chinese were allowed into the country each year.

In 1965 all quota systems were abolished. Chinese could finally enter America together as families. Still, many paper sons and their descendants worried they'd get sent back to China if anyone found out about their past. Today, though, younger generations are trying to find information about their families, wanting to learn about, share, and celebrate their stories.

Maizy, in your email you said that the laws didn't seem fair. I agree! Just because there are laws doesn't mean they are right. In 2017, the president banned many Muslims and stopped thousands of refugees— people who are forced to leave their country because they were being unfairly punished—from coming to the United States. During the Holocaust, it was illegal to hide Jews. Slavery was legal in America, and entire Native American communities were slaughtered in the name of patriotism. We should never forget these wrongs.

I know that anti-immigrant rhetoric and anti-Asian crimes are scary. That's why it's so important to talk about them. We can't pretend that bad things didn't happen in the past and aren't happening now. But we can address them and shine a light on the problems while looking for solutions. I am so sorry to hear about Bud the Bear, and, yes, the threatening note makes it a hate crime. I hope he'll be found soon, along with the coward who left the anoymous note.

—Emmy

P.S. Keep those questions coming. In return, I look forward to hearing more about the Golden Palace and Lucky.

I write back to Emmy about Lucky and include a list of paper son names that were on the photos and in the letters. From my research, I learned that people took on new names to match the immigration documents. Lots of families lost track of relatives who gave up one name and life for another.

Is finding Last Chance's paper sons an impossible dream?

When I get home, I ask, "Opa, why did Lucky return to San Francisco? Why do people go back to places when they don't know if they'll be welcomed?"

When we drove to Last Chance, the closer we got, the harder Mom gripped the steering wheel. "Are you okay?" I asked.

"I guess we'll find out," she said.

Opa mutes the television. "Like in poker, people weigh their odds and take risks. They want to know how the game will play out."

Home

1891

Mr. Philips was grayer than before but had the same smile. "Lucky . . . is that really you?!"

"It's good to see you," Mrs. Philips added.

"Please." Lucky launched into the speech he had been practicing since the day he fled San Francisco. "There is something I need to tell you—"

"First, there is something we need to tell you," Mr. Philips interrupted. "We know you didn't steal from us."

Lucky was stunned. "You know?"

"Yes." Mrs. Philips said. "We found the watch in Jenkins's room. And that policeman tried to sell my earrings and other jewels. Imagine that!"

Lucky gasped. He felt like he had been underwater for fifteen years and finally reached the surface.

"We searched for you. Where did you go?" Mr. Philips asked.

"Minnesota. I own a restaurant there," Lucky said proudly.

"Sell the restaurant and come back to us!" Mr. Philips looked pleased with his idea.

Just then the Chinese housekeeper arrived with a tray of tea and sweets. She and Lucky stole glances at each other.

Lucky was distracted. "Excuse me, what did you say?"

"Give yourself a couple of weeks to think it over," Mr. Philips suggested. "We'd love to have you back in our house."

"Please stop by while you're deciding," Mrs. Philips told him.

Lucky came by the Philips Mansion every day for the next two weeks. It was hard deciding whether to stay in Last Chance or accept Mr. Philips's offer. When the two weeks were up, the train trip was far more enjoyable than the last time he had left San Francisco. This time, Lucky was going home.

Chapter 44

The entrance looks so empty without Bud. Every morning Logan meets me at the Golden Palace before we begin our search.

"Bud, where are you?!" We don't care who hears us. In fact, I hope whoever took him knows that we're not going to stop looking until Bud's home safe.

Searching for a wooden bear can be exhausting. Now we're sharing a banana split at Ben Franklin. Logan doesn't eat fruits or vegetables, so the banana, strawberry, and pineapple toppings and maraschino cherries are mine.

I take out a copy of the ransom note. "The handwriting is sloppy. It says 'We have ur bear,' not 'I have your bear.'"

"So you think it's a gang of criminals?" Logan has eaten all the chocolate ice cream and is now starting on the vanilla.

"Yes. Besides, Bud is too big for one person to carry." I set the cherries aside to eat last. Eva always gives me extra. "I think it's a prank. If it was a real kidnapping, they would have contacted us by now. I wish there was a way we could compare everyone's handwriting and—"

Before I even finish my sentence, Logan leaps up. "A petition! If we have a petition, we can get signatures."

"Great idea!" I wish I had thought of that. "What will the petition be for?"

Chapter 45

I'm hiding behind the mailbox. If whoever wrote the note sees me, they might figure out why I'd want their signature. Opa's binoculars have come in handy.

Daisy is in tears. Logan can make his voice crack at the same point every time. ". . . without our support, the innocent gray wolves could become extinct and die."

I don't tell him that if they are extinct, it means they're all already dead.

Daisy's purse is one of those floppy bags made from old jeans. She signs her name, then hands Logan a crumpled five-dollar bill. "For the baby wolves."

So far we've gathered fifteen signatures. It would be more, but some people turn around when they see Logan running toward them. When he spots Riley down the street, he calls her name.

She doesn't hesitate to sign the petition, and when Riley asks him "How can I help?" Logan is too stunned to speak.

I may have misjudged her. I come out of hiding. She's not the enemy. Riley nods as I tell her about the ransom note, and add, "More people might be willing to sign a petition if you're asking."

Just then I hear loud voices. I duck behind the mailbox.

Logan waves to Erik, who's with a boy who looks happy just to be in his orbit.

"Save the gray wolves!" Logan says.

Erik grabs the clipboard and tosses it to his sidekick. "Why would I want to do that? It's—"

Before he can finish, someone yells, "Erik Fisk, stop teasing that little boy!"

I train the binoculars on a solid-looking woman marching down the street. Her purse is the size of a small suitcase.

"Hey, Mom." Erik flashes a megawatt smile.

"Mrs. Fisk, won't you help save the gray wolves?" Riley asks.

Logan launches into his speech. "They are so rare that other wolves think of them as royalty."

Mrs. Fisk fans her face. "I adore the royal family, all that pomp," she tells Riley even though Logan is still talking. She signs and passes the clipboard to Erik. "Your compassion for baby animals does not go unnoticed," Mrs. Fisk commends Riley. "You are a credit to our town."

"You're welcome!" Logan calls out as they leave.

I take out the ransom note and compare it to the petition. Erik's handwriting doesn't match, and neither does anyone else's.

Chapter 46

I'm using a piece of cardboard to wave away the smoke. The vent in Werner's kitchen can only do so much.

"Germans are the biggest immigrant group in Minnesota." Werner's brats are always perfectly grilled, giving them a snap when you bite down. "Every summer when my mother went to the old country to visit my oma and opa, she would bring me back one of these." He points to the snow globes crowding a shelf.

I examine one that features a pair of dancing pigs. "That one was your grandpa's favorite when we were kids," Werner says. "He took it once, but when his mother found out, she dragged him back here and made him confess."

I start laughing. This doesn't surprise me.

"You called your grandparents Opa and Oma, too?" I ask. "Isn't that Chinese?"

"Actually, it's German." Werner turns his impressive nose upward, sniffing the air like Lazy Dog. "Black bean fish fillets!"

The two old men have started making special requests.

Werner is partial to the Golden Palace's savory dishes. "I've never met a chili pepper that I didn't like," he says.

Opa's favorite bratwurst comes with grilled onions, chunky brown mustard, and sauerkraut. He never finishes one anymore, but he still loves it when I bring them home. I feel like a delivery service. I don't mind. When Werner opens his fortune cookie today, he'll read, Great food and great friendships are meant to be enjoyed.

Opa is getting the same one.

Werner didn't take Bud. But I already knew that.

When I get home, I ask, "Is 'opa' how they say 'grandfather' in China?"

Opa shakes his head. "No, it's German, and it's also Dutch. In Chinese, 'grandfather' is 'gung gung' and 'grandmother' is 'po po.'"

"Then why are you and Grandma 'Opa' and 'Oma'?"

"My grandfather Lucky wanted to be accepted by white people so badly. When I was born, I was delivered by a German midwife. She looked white. So, when she referred to the new grandparents as Opa and Oma, Lucky embraced that, thinking it was what Americans called their grandfathers and grandmothers."

I nod and take a bite of my brat. "Speaking of Lucky," I say, "what happened when he left San Francisco and returned to Last Chance?"

Big News

1891

The news traveled fast around Last Chance. Lucky was back! Outside the Golden Grille, a sign read: *Open Today for Lunch.* At precisely noon, Lucky swung open the door.

"Lucky!" Happy was in tears. "You're not dead!"

Calls of "Welcome back!" and "We missed you" warmed Lucky's heart.

"It is so good to be home." He hesitated, then cleared his throat for a big announcement. "I'd like you to meet my new business partner!"

The crowd stared in disbelief.

"This is Lulu," Lucky said, beaming. "She's also my bride."

Standing next to Bud the Bear, the Chinese woman looked small. But soon enough, the town learned of her oversized personality and heart.

Business was great. Customers came in for the food, but stayed to talk to Lulu. She always made time to listen to customers' stories and could make anyone feel at home.

Lucky was happy to have Lulu by his side, but he worried that Last Chance was not nearly as glamorous as San Francisco. The newlyweds hadn't even had time for a honeymoon.

"I am so sorry."

"For what?" Lulu was scrubbing the floor.

"For making you leave San Francisco. For making you work day and night." Lucky felt ashamed. "The Golden Grille can't compare to the Philips Mansion."

Lulu stood up. "You are right. This can't compare. This isn't a mansion."

Lucky looked pained until his wife took his hands in hers. "This is a palace and it's all ours."

The next week the Golden Grille sign came down. In its place, a new one went up: *Golden Palace.*

Chapter 47

"Commercials are like thirty-second stories, and in the ones I work on, the food is the hero," Mom is telling Opa.

Before I take off, I hear her describing how cardboard is slid under each layer of pancakes to keep them from caving in.

When Opa declares, "You're a sly one, Charlotte!" Mom looks like she's just been awarded the prize for Best Butter Cow.

Since my mother is spending the day with Opa, I head to the restaurant to help out. Before I go in, I face the empty spot where Bud should be, and I look up at the sign. You can tell that it's been painted over a lot. The colors may have changed, but the Golden Palace name remains the same.

In the kitchen, Daisy blanches baby bok choy to stir-fry with oyster sauce.

"I like your earrings," I tell her. They're made from bottle caps.

Daisy absentmindedly touches them. "More than eighty percent of a mattress can be recycled," she says.

In the office, I say hello to the paper sons photos. Lynn Fong from New Jersey has been emailing me about her ancestry search. After her grandfather Eddie Fong spent a summer in Last Chance, she traced his journey to New York, where he worked in a Chinese restaurant. Eventually, Eddie owned a dim sum shop. *I like to think his love of the restaurant business was inspired by Lucky,* she wrote.

Emmy says that she posted a "Last Chance Paper Sons" inquiry online and it's garnering some interest. She's going to review the comments before forwarding them to me. Maybe I can help connect the dots for other people, too.

When I wander into the dining room, Oma is chatting with Lady Macbeth. Nearby, Principal Holmes is enjoying his noodles when some kids run over and ask him about the sloth wearing sunglasses on his T-shirt. They keep talking until their parents call them back to their table.

The other night I asked Mom, "What do you think of Principal Holmes?"

"I love him," she said without hesitation.

"Love" is a pretty strong word. I think about Oma and Opa.

The colorful blanket Opa keeps draped over his knees was made by Werner's wife. Werner told me, "Delores was featured in *Minnesota Dontcha Know* when she knit a sweater for a horse."

Werner is a big man with a booming voice, but when he talks about his wife, his tone turns gentle. Oma and Opa bicker all the time, but you can tell they love each other. I wonder if my mother ever had someone who loved her like that. There was one boyfriend who drove a fancy sports car and called me Miss Maze, and that one who was always eating mints. But the only man I've ever seen her truly happy with is Principal Holmes.

Chapter 48

Mom is cleaning out the refrigerator. There are lots of leftovers, since Opa hasn't been eating much. On TV, Carlos! is in Atkins, Arkansas, passing out deep-fried pickles. Oma looks tiny curled up on the couch. Opa is in his wheelchair next to her. When they cut to a commercial, my grandfather perks up. "Charlotte's french fries!"

Mom can't hide her delight when the golden french fries tumble down in slow motion on-screen. A light dusting of salt falls like fresh winter snow. The music swells as the camera pans to the fries lovingly arranged in a familiar red paper holder with golden arches.

Opa claps and I cheer. Oma shakes her head. "You go to college and end up faking food?"

Mom stiffens. "I was a film major. A food stylist needs to know about lighting and camera angles, and color. I've worked on six Clio Award winners!"

"That's like the Academy Awards, only for commercials," I tell Opa.

"So you did," Oma reluctantly admits. "I loved college," she adds wistfully.

"Oma, you went to college?" This surprises me.

"Where do you think I found that one?" She points to Opa.

"That grouchy lady was the only other Chinese student." He motions to Oma. "Everyone kept trying to push us together, but she refused to even look at me. So stubborn!"

"So how did you end up with each other?" I ask. Mom looks interested, too.

Opa now points to himself. "This face is irresistible! Once your grandmother got her snooty nose out of the air to get a good look at my handsome mug, she started chasing me."

I wait for Oma to deny it, but instead she says, "It's true! Look at him, still so handsome. We married right after graduation and were set to honeymoon in Hawaii."

They beam at each other, and I don't see a sick old man in a wheelchair or a tired elderly woman who's worried about him. Instead, I see a young couple on the beach admiring the sunset.

Opa reaches for Oma. When they hold hands, his don't shake. "We never got to Hawaii." Regret settles on his face. "My father had a heart attack right after the wedding and passed away."

Oma nods. "Instead of going to Hawaii, we honeymooned at the Golden Palace."

For the first time since I got here, Opa looks like he's in pain. "I'm so sorry."

"I'm not," Oma insists, squeezing his hand.

Tears escape from her eyes, and Mom and I look at each other helplessly. I've never seen my grandmother cry.

"Old lady, stop those waterworks!" Opa orders. "Save it for my funeral!"

Oma wipes her face with the back of her hand. "You make me so mad sometimes," she snaps. "Don't say things like that."

"If you use up all your tears now, you won't have any left for when I'm dead and buried," he jokes.

"That's not funny," Oma says as she looks away.

Chapter 49

It's Monday. The Noisy Family is back. The mother is clearly exhausted. Do all moms look like that? I know she loves our egg rolls, so I bring her an extra one on the house. That's when I spot Mom greeting Principal Holmes. Today's T-shirt says: *So Many Books, So Little Time.*

"Kung pao shrimp today?"

"You know me well, Char."

A quiet smile passes between them, but I see it. I know that he'd never steal Bud or do anything that would upset my mother.

Mom lowers her voice. What are they saying to each other that's so private? I stand around the corner to listen in.

"I'm not sure if I can do this—"

When Principal Holmes takes her hands in his, I leave.

He isn't that bad. They can't get too serious, though, because then we'd be stuck in Last Chance. I wonder if I can talk Principal Holmes into moving to Los Angeles. I guess it would be okay if they dated.

Later, I ask Oma, "What's with Mom and Principal Holmes?"

"Best friends since they were little." She tosses a handful of peanuts into the stir-fry.

I count four extra shrimp in Principal Holmes's order.

"What do you think of him?"

"Who, Glenn? He's like family." The garlic sizzles as the shrimp turn from gray to white. "He had a rough time growing up. I think he got along better with me and Opa than his own parents."

I wonder if Oma wishes that Mom married Principal Holmes and had a baby with him. In the office, I type up some fortunes like, Friends and family are always welcome here.

I scoop rice into a bowl and pack it down with the back of a spoon, then turn it upside down on the plate. When I lift it up, there's a perfect dome of rice. I place the fortune cookie next to the shrimp and the bowl of wonton soup.

"Our customers love your fortunes." Oma winks at me.

I smile back and pick up the tray. "Do you think Principal Holmes and Mom will get together? You know, like dating or whatever?"

Oma is still for a moment. Her voice softens. "I don't think so. They're best friends who've reconnected and are enjoying being back with each other."

She didn't see them whisper or hold hands.

Is now the time to ask about another pair of best friends? I've been wondering what happened between Opa and

Werner for months. I'm about to bring it up when Finn, the little kid Logan gives worms to, barges into the dining room, waving a flyer.

"Maizy, I found him! I found Bud the Bear—"

It's hard to keep up with Finn. Lazy Dog surprises me by joining us. The three of us race toward the train depot. Logan is at the wishing well.

"Bud is in the woods!" Finn yells to him.

We're all out of breath when Finn finally slows. We're surrounded by trees, but there's no sign of a bear. "Well?" I ask.

"Bud was just here!" He looks uncertain.

"Where?" Logan presses. "We've looked in this area dozens of times."

Finn can't recall the exact spot where he saw Bud. We keep looking at the same places over and over again.

"Maybe it's time to head back," I tell Finn. It's starting to get dark. "Bud's not here."

"No, wait, I know he's close," he insists. "I saw him!"

"Maizy's right," Logan adds, looking at me. I know we're both thinking that Finn really didn't see Bud.

I've just wasted hours. We're about to leave when Lazy Dog starts barking. Finn gasps. Tiny golden lights dart past us. We follow the fireflies. There, just off the path, I see him.

"Bud!" I stumble down the small embankment, skinning my knee. "Are you okay?" I ask. I can't believe I'm crying.

Bud is on his back as if he's taking a nap. Part of his left paw is broken, but otherwise he seems fine. I notice two small holes in his shoulder and one in his chest. A bullet from Lucky's days is still lodged in one of them.

"IT'S BUD! WE FOUND BUD!" Logan yells.

"See, I told you!" Finn shouts. "I'm good at finding things. I found my uncle's dentures in the garbage once. I get the reward, right?"

Chapter 50

The first person I tell is Opa. "Long live Bud!" he cries, raising his lemonade into the air.

I haven't seen him this happy in a long time. Our luck is on the rise.

"Maizy, are you sure you can find him again in the morning?" Opa asks.

I nod. "I left behind a trail of poker chips, just like in 'Hansel and Gretel'!"

Opa laughs. "People think cats have nine lives, but what they don't know is that bears do, too."

My next stop is the restaurant. Oma is overjoyed. Daisy cries. Principal Holmes says that he can fix Bud's paw. Eva offers her truck, and Mom assures me, "We will get Bud first thing in the morning when there's daylight. I promise!"

I'm lingering in the restaurant lobby when Mayor Whitlock motions me over to his table. He looks troubled. "Did I hear correctly? You found Bud?!"

Lady Macbeth sips her tea slowly as she listens in.

"Yes, so I guess you interviewed me for nothing."

"It's a solid article. Award-worthy, even. Though it had more punch when Bud was still missing," Mayor Whitlock says, more to himself than to me. "It's not due for a couple days, so I still have time to rewrite the ending. Maizy, did you find out who left the ransom note?"

I shake my head. Whoever did it is still out there. I saw a whiskey bottle near Bud. Maybe that's a clue?

In the morning, a small crowd has gathered. Logan shouts, "Everyone, stand back so we can get Bud!"

Finn pokes me and whispers, "Tell 'em it was me who found the bear!"

The hardware store owner brings a rope to hoist Bud up, and several people, including Mom, Werner, and Principal Holmes, carry Bud up the embankment to Eva's truck while Mayor Whitlock takes photos. Erik and Sidekick and the Mean Girls are here, along with some people I don't recognize. Riley waves to me.

It's a short drive down Main Street, and when Eva pulls up in front of the Golden Palace, Oma and Opa are waiting outside. It's the first time he's been out of the house in a week.

"Bud!" Daisy cries, jumping up and down.

Everyone cheers when he's back in front of the Golden Palace where he belongs. Opa wheels up and pats his paw.

Oma cleans off the dirt and leaves on Bud. Lazy Dog curls up next to the bear as if he's guarding him.

"Can I get my reward now?" Finn asks eagerly. "Maizy says I can eat here for a week for free!"

Oma nods. "Anything you want."

"Wheel me into the restaurant," Opa tells Finn, "and prepare for the biggest feast of your life!"

He's in such a great mood, my grandfather will agree to anything. "Lucky Story tonight?" I ask.

"You betcha!" Opa promises.

Today is a good day.

Paper Sons

1905

Seven days a week, Lucky and Lulu worked day and night. With the train stopping in Last Chance, the Golden Palace was the perfect place for travelers to get a good meal. But it wasn't just white people who were disembarking at the depot.

When Lucky was in San Francisco's Chinatown, most people couldn't even imagine a Chinese restaurant in the middle of America. Still, they were impressed with Lucky. By then, the boy from Guangdong, China, had been in the United States for over thirty years.

The Chinese Exclusion Act still kept immigrants from becoming citizens. However, many had purchased documents declaring them to be the son of an American citizen, and therefore granting them citizenship.

Lucky wasn't a paper son. He came to America before the exclusion law was enacted. But he never forgot how hard it was when he first arrived. He told other immigrants, "If you find yourself in Minnesota, come see me if you need help or just want a good meal."

With trains branching out across the country, it wasn't

uncommon for a paper son to knock on the back door of the Golden Palace. Word among the Chinese community was that there was a man in the middle of the country who welcomed strangers and didn't ask a lot of questions. Lulu had benefited from the help of Mrs. Philips and was determined to do the same for others. "Though we have just met, you are family here," she told the visitors.

By then, the Chens were living in a small house close by. Off the restaurant kitchen was a back office, where their guests slept. There, Lulu began putting up photos and notes from their visitors. Some stayed a couple of nights. Others stayed a week or so, and a few stayed for months. Everyone worked in the kitchen and was careful not to be seen, or else Lucky and Lulu might get in trouble. After all, the hatred toward Chinese was still high.

It wasn't just Chinese immigrants who benefited from the help of the Golden Palace's owners. Lulu, especially, assisted locals, taking food to widows and families in need. Some referred to her as an angel, though not all.

"Go home to China," they'd say.

More than once Bud the Bear was pushed over.

One night, after an especially long day, there was pounding on the door of Lucky and Lulu's house. It was the paper son who had been working for them. "Fire!" he yelled in Chinese.

Again, the fire brigade assembled to put out the flames. Only this time, the damage was much worse than before.

"Arson." Sheriff Swain shook his head as he looked at the

Golden Palace's charred walls and burnt furniture the next morning.

Lucky couldn't believe this had happened a second time. "Maybe we should go back to San Francisco." He sounded defeated. "We could work for the Philipses—or even go back to China."

"China?" Lulu was stunned. "I'm an American. I can't even speak Chinese!"

Lucky motioned to a smoldering pile of wood. "But this."

"If we left, the cowards who did this would win," Lulu said. "Besides, what would we tell our child?"

Lucky looked confused. "Our child?"

Lulu put her hand on her belly and laughed. It was the only time she had ever seen Lucky speechless.

Chapter 51

Daisy is stressed. She's in charge of the banana leaves.

"You add a bit of salted fish in the middle of the pork, then wrap like this," Oma says, showing her. "We use banana, since we don't have taro leaves."

Even though the laulau is being served at dinner, it can take hours to steam. This gives us enough time to transform the Golden Palace into as close to a Hawaiian paradise as we can.

My mother is putting ocean-scented candles on each table and sprinkling shells around them. I put a couple of them in my fishing vest. "Have they always done this?" I ask as I finish hanging the strands of small twinkling lights. They remind me of fireflies.

Oma approaches, holding an armful of colorful paper leis. "We couldn't get to Hawaii for our honeymoon, so we bring Hawaii here once a year for our wedding anniversary."

That reminds me. I run to the office to get the flowers that Opa ordered.

Oma tries to look angry, but I can tell she's thrilled.

"Every year, he spends too much money on these!" Slowly, she opens the box.

"Here, let me help you," Mom says, putting the purple-and-white lei around Oma's neck.

The three of us pause to take in the sweet scent of the orchids. The moment is broken when Daisy calls out, "How long do I cook the salmon?"

In a flash, Oma rushes into the kitchen. Diced tomatoes and onions are ready to add to the small squares of raw salmon. "Lomi lomi is meant to be eaten raw, like sushi," she says, guiding Daisy away from the stove.

Back home, my grandfather is waiting for me. He's wearing a Hawaiian shirt and acting like his old self. "Take me to my bride!" he orders. Opa's not supposed to go out, but his doctor gave permission for this one night.

Bud's been back for a few days now. He greets us with a stack of leis around his neck and has several more hanging off each arm. A sign in Oma's writing says: *Welcome to Hawaii Night—Take One.*

Opa takes three. I take two.

Inside, twinkling lights and candlelit tables make it look like a fairyland. There's an album on the record player, and a man is singing a Hawaiian song about "tiny bubbles."

Oma comes over to Opa. "Aloha!" Over his paper leis, she places one made of leaves around his neck.

Mom brings out a platter with laulau and poi, a dish that

looks like purple pudding. When she places the lomi lomi in front of Opa, Daisy hurries out of the kitchen and explains, "I didn't forget to cook it. It's supposed to be raw, like sushi."

She's almost back in the kitchen when Opa yells, "Daisy, stop!"

Trembling, she faces my grandfather, who points to the lomi lomi. "Delish dish!" he announces, to her relief.

Oma is greeting all the customers with a warm "Welcome to Hawaii Night." Principal Holmes shows up in a vintage *Surf's Up* T-shirt, and Lady Macbeth's dress has a festive flower pattern on it. Everyone wishes Oma and Opa a happy anniversary.

Now Don Ho, the man on the album cover, is singing, *"Of sweet aloha . . . I will love you longer than forever . . ."*

Mom confides, "When I was growing up, every year they'd dance to this song in the middle of the restaurant. I was so embarrassed." She shakes her head. "I wish they could dance now."

Without thinking, I rush over and whisper to Opa, then Oma. When Mom sees what's happening, she lifts the record player needle and starts the song over again. Then I slowly whirl my grandparents around as Oma sits on Opa's lap and Don Ho serenades them with "Hawaiian Wedding Song."

Chapter 52

Opa has been having trouble shuffling the cards. He's not nearly as energetic as he was that night of their anniversary. When he drops the deck, we both laugh and pretend he did it on purpose. "That's what we call fifty-two-card pickup," he jokes. "There are now fifty-two cards on the floor for you to pick up!"

I can't believe how far some of the cards flew. "Be sure to get every single one," Opa says. "Otherwise it's a fouled deck."

"What's that?" When I reach under the couch, in addition to the ace of spades, I also find a golf ball and a half-empty box of cigarettes.

"A fouled deck is when there's something wrong, like some cards are missing." Opa gazes at the cigarettes before declaring, "Not mine. Anyway, you can't play a true game of poker with a fouled deck."

After I gather the fifty-two cards, I take the brats out of the bag. Opa starts eating the triple-alarm hot chili pepper bratwurst that I got for myself. That's when I remember he can't do spicy anymore. It makes him sick. "Opa!"

"What?" he asks with his mouth full.

Opa would never admit it, but his taste buds must be gone. Mom says this happens to older people. I take the spicy brat and place a bowl of wonton soup in front of him. "Did Werner accuse you of cheating at poker?"

Instantly, he puts on his poker face. "Who told you that?"

"Oma."

Opa picks up the Chinese ceramic soup spoon with a blue flower painted in the center. He stirs the soup and considers my question like he's just been dealt some new cards.

"What Werner thinks and what is true may be two different things." His hand shakes, causing the soup to spill.

Wordlessly, I replace the spoon with a mild bratwurst in a bun. It's big enough, and soft enough, so Opa can grip it. "Well, did you cheat?"

"So what if I did?" Opa is delighted by the shocked look on my face. "I'd have to be dead before I admit it! Besides, it was just that one time, and he made such a big fuss over nothing."

Werner has just arrived. When he sees Opa, Werner's already sad face looks even sadder. The two former best friends watch in silence as Carlos! is surrounded by college students from Northampton, Massachusetts.

"The crust is flaky!" Carlos! holds the pastry tart aloft. The students cheer like they're at a football game. "The lemon tangy!" Louder cheers. "And the meringue so sweet I want to marry it! This is a . . ."

Swept up in the excitement, the college students and Opa and Werner all yell "Delish dish" along with Carlos! Opa and Werner accidentally grin at each other before remembering that they are sworn enemies.

Chapter 53

It's been almost a week since Finn found Bud. For someone so skinny, he sure orders a lot of food. You'd think he doesn't eat much at home.

"Thanks, Mrs. Chen," Finn says when Oma gives him big bags of food to go.

"We accidentally made too much again," she explains.

Logan and I are headed to the train depot when a pack of teenagers push their way out of Ben Franklin. I recognize Erik and shove Logan into the doorway so we can hide.

"What?!" he says.

I motion to the teens.

"The church at midnight," Erik's ordering his friends. "Unless you're a coward!"

"Keep your eyes on your opponent," Opa always tells me. "The ones who are the loudest are often making up for their weak cards."

"Maybe we'll even visit our buddy again," Erik says as Sidekick nods.

When Logan starts to complain, I elbow him.

"Criminals always return to the scene of their crimes," I whisper. "I think Erik's going to do something to Bud again tonight!"

"His handwriting didn't match," Logan reminds me.

"Maybe one of the others wrote it," I say as the group makes their way down Main Street.

It's 11:30 p.m. Logan is too chicken to sneak out, so I'm going solo. I slip on Opa's fishing vest. Mom's old Polaroid camera fits in one of the huge pockets, along with a flashlight, binoculars, and other supplies.

Except for Carlos! on TV, everyone in the house is asleep. "We're at an Asian market in Oakland, California." Carlos! holds up a dangerous-looking spiky fruit. "The durian has such a pungent smell that it's banned on public transportation in Singapore. . . ."

The streets are empty. Crickets chirp. Lazy Dog is trotting around, sniffing here and there. He doesn't seem so lazy at night. Old-fashioned streetlamps illuminate Main Street, so I stay in the shadows. The Golden Palace is up ahead on the corner. I can make out Bud's silhouette.

11:45 p.m. I'm the first one at the church. It's kind of scary here. I slip easily under the uneven wooden stairs at the side of the building. Being small has its benefits.

At 12:08 a.m., a low murmur makes its way toward me. My entire body tenses as the voices get louder, more excited. The boys are laughing and ordering each other to be quiet. Sidekick is gripping a brown paper bag.

"Let's get this party rolling!" Erik orders.

I remain unseen as they snake past me. Then, in total spy mode, I follow, silent as a cat.

Their shadows look gigantic by the light of the moon. I resist taking a photo. I've only got one shot, since the flash would give me away. One photo and run—that's the plan. Then I'll have my proof!

Their voices are amplified in the darkness. "I get the first swig, but who wants the second?"

Swig?

I adjust the binoculars.

"Great whiskey!" Erik whistles appreciatively.

Whiskey?! There was a bottle of whiskey by Bud when we found him. I lean back into the shadows. The boys keep passing the bottle, and I settle in for what could be a long night.

Two hours later, they're a group of stupid drunk teenagers. They stagger through town like toddlers learning to walk. When they split up, I figure everyone's going home. I'm tired and can't wait to get into bed.

I'm nearing the Golden Palace when I hear yelling. Suddenly I'm wide awake. There's no time to be afraid. I run faster than I thought was possible. There! Over where Bud stands, I spot a figure in the shadows. My hands are shaking as I reach for the Polaroid. I aim and press the button. For a split second, the flash lights up the person next to Bud.

"Hey!"

"You?" I say, stunned as the camera spits out a photo.

Chapter 54

I can't stop my body from shaking.

"Maizy?!"

My mother looks shocked. "Do you have any idea what time it is? Are you okay? Why did you run away? Did you just take my picture?"

The questions bounce off me. All I can do is stare at Bud. Someone wrote *Chink!* on him.

All at once I feel angry, scared, and confused.

"Mom?" I feel like throwing up. She's holding a brush dripping with yellow paint. My voice quakes as I point. "Did you do that?"

"Do what?" She startles when she sees the graffiti on Bud. "No!" Mom tosses the paintbrush like it's on fire. "How could you even ask that? I was looking for you, when I saw someone. . . . I shouted 'STOP!' They dropped this and ran."

There's an open can of paint on the ground.

I'm flooded with relief, but then seconds later a surge of adrenaline hits me so hard I almost lose my balance. "Who was it?" I grab Mom's arm. "Come on, let's go! They can't be too far away—"

"Maizy Chen!" She doesn't budge. "I didn't see who it was. And even if I did, we're not about to go running around in the dark. It's not safe. Besides, you have some explaining to do."

Chapter 55

Last night Mom was so mad. She gave me a speech about safety that went on forever. Then Oma jumped in and began lecturing—then Mom again. It went back and forth like that for what seemed like forever. Even though I apologized about a hundred times, I doubt either one of them heard me. I'm grounded for sneaking out and only allowed to be at the Golden Palace or with my grandfather. Right now Oma's at home with Opa. Both are shaken up by what's happened to Bud, though neither will admit it.

My fishing vest is stained with yellow. I used it to try to wipe the paint off, but only managed to smear the slur. Principal Holmes shows up with solvent to remove the paint. By lunchtime, the word is gone from Bud, but not from my memory.

Mayor Whitlock is adding sugar to his tea. "Who would have thought this sort of thing could happen in Last Chance?" he says as I walk past.

We both know what he's talking about.

"Not me." That's for sure.

Back in the kitchen, Daisy studies the mayor. She walks toward him and turns around so many times, it looks like a dance.

"I want to talk to him about recycling." Daisy is wearing her rice bag dress and button necklace for good luck. "But he looks so scary."

I sneak a peek at Mayor Whitlock, who's just dipped a napkin into his water and is trying to mop up the tea he spilled on his shirt.

"Maizy, what should I do?"

I hand her a fortune cookie.

She reads the slip of paper, nods, straightens, and marches into the dining room.

I can't hear them talking, but after a few minutes, Daisy waltzes back to the kitchen with flushed cheeks. "My fortune cookie told me to take a chance. So I did . . . and Mayor Whitlock promised to consider a Last Chance recycling program!"

Sometimes all someone needs is a little nudge.

Chapter 56

When I join Opa for lunch, I finally manage to pick up a single grain of rice with my chopsticks.

"You're a real Chinese girl now," Opa congratulates me. He pushes a full bowl of rice across the table. "Here's the present I promised you!"

"Opa!" I cry. It feels good to laugh instead of thinking about the hate speech written on Bud.

Carlos! is about to eat escargot at a French bistro. "Those are snails," Opa says, pointing to the television. "Hey, Carlos! Slow down!"

"Why were they all men?" I ask. I've been wondering this for a while.

"The snails?"

"The photos on the office wall. Were there any paper daughters?"

Opa turns down the television volume. "Back then, women were expected to stay in China and take care of their in-laws."

I remember Lucky's uncle thinking that girls weren't

worth as much as boys. This makes me mad! "In school, we learned that women couldn't even vote in America until a hundred years ago. Why is the world so messed up?"

He shakes his head. "I wish I knew. You know, Chinese Americans didn't have the right to vote until 1943. That means Lucky was ninety the first time he cast a ballot."

"So then it was double as hard for Chinese women in America?"

"You could say that. Some women were sent for when their husbands were financially secure. Very few came on their own. It would have been very dangerous. But if you look carefully, you may find one brave paper daughter on our wall."

What? This can't be. I've memorized all the faces and they're all male.

Opa gets the look he has when he's about to tell me a Lucky Story, only this one isn't about my great-great-grandfather. . . .

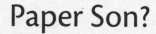

Paper Son?

1935

Before I was born, a young man came to work at the Golden Palace for a few short weeks. My mother, Ana, recalled that with his soft features and smooth face, he looked like a child. My father, Philip, said this little fellow could imitate anyone and was always keeping them entertained.

His name was Jian Lee, and he was passing through on his way to the West Coast. In those days, some paper sons were heading to the East Coast, and others were heading to the West Coast. Either way, some ended up in Minnesota during their journey.

One late night after work, my mother went to the Golden Palace to get a dress she had ordered from the Sears catalog. She was going to wear it to church the next morning. But when she got to the restaurant, Jian was gone. Instead, she saw a beautiful young Chinese woman trying on the dress. My mother was shocked, not knowing where she'd come from.

The young woman was flustered to have been caught, but she trusted my mother. She had come to know her goodness over the past couple of weeks. Over a pot of tea, the stranger told an incredible story—that she was masquerading as Jian Lee.

Her parents had put up their life savings to send her only brother to America as a paper son. Tragically, he fell ill and died before the ship sailed. Unable to get their money back, the girl, who was barely a teenager, went in his place. Only, she had to pretend to be her brother, who was pretending to be another person himself.

After Last Chance, Jian eventually made it to Hollywood. She changed her name to Jean Lee and became one of the first Chinese actresses in American movies. When pressed about her background, she'd reluctantly reveal her secret identity . . . as a Chinese princess. People wanted to believe her, so they did.

My mother never told my father or Lucky or Lulu this secret, but before she died, she told me Jean Lee's story. "Johnny," she told me, "things aren't always what they seem. The same goes for people."

Chapter 57

I'm not grounded anymore! Before I meet up with Logan, I stop at the Golden Palace to look for Jean Lee. I examine each picture closely, but she's not there. Is Opa teasing me again? Then I remember to "read the table."

I back away from the wall and take all the pictures in at once. So many serious faces—but one does not look like the others. Slowly, I move in, letting the other pictures fade as this one comes into focus. . . .

I see a young man with a soft face and smooth skin. But more than that, he's laughing like he has a secret—and the secret is that it's Jean Lee disguised as her brother, Jian Lee.

Hello, paper daughter.

"Sweet with a slight garlic bite and tinge of red pepper," I tell Opa when I get home. His eyes are closed as I describe some of the dishes Lady Macbeth ordered. His appetite may have abandoned him, but his love of food hasn't.

"Go on, Maizy."

"The beef is braised the way you like it"—the look of satisfaction on his face makes me happy—"so tender that it's falling apart, and the gai lan has just a touch of oyster sauce. . . ."

When I'm done, Opa sighs happily. He opens his eyes and rearranges the Delores blanket. Even though it's summer, he gets cold.

"That was like hearing about old friends. You think you know them, but they can surprise you."

I nod, remembering when I found out that Principal Holmes sang in a barbershop quartet.

"Oma told Daisy that food can be familiar and unexpected at the same time," I say. "It's sort of like that."

"Yes, yes!" he agrees. "It's the Chinese philosophy of yin and yang, where what appears to be contrary may be complementary. Sometimes when opposites work together, everything becomes stronger, better."

This makes me think of the dishes Oma cooks. Lately, Mom's been styling them with small touches, like fresh curls of carrots and radish roses. It makes what was already great even better.

Werner doesn't even knock. Instead, he just comes in and stays for hours. Sometimes he even closes his restaurant early so he can spend more time with Opa before Oma comes home. They're still not speaking to each other, but both will talk to Carlos!

"That barbecue brisket looks perfect," Werner will say.

"You're right, Carlos! It doesn't need to be drenched in sauce. Let the flavor come through!" Opa will add without looking at Werner.

Everyone tries to avoid the obvious—that my grand-father's illness is getting worse. Mom and Oma chatter about difficult customers and Daisy's compost pile. It's the sorrow-ful silence that's awkward, so they talk nonstop.

"Stop with the yammering," Opa orders. He winks at me, but even that seems hard for him to do. "So, if I die, I die!"

I wince.

"Shush, old man!" Oma looks pained.

"Dad! Really," Mom scolds. "How can you say that?"

Oma and my mother are united in anger and love. The bond is so tight that sometimes I can't tell the difference.

"Because it's true?" my grandfather answers.

Werner sits quietly in the corner looking like he's going to cry. His tell is way off. If this is how he plays poker, then Opa must have beat him every time. When Werner catches me watching him, he puts on his poker face and I put on mine.

Chapter 58

M om and I are walking to the Golden Palace to get ready for opening. Oma has been spending more time at home. She's started sleeping downstairs to be near Opa.

"What does the doctor say?" I ask. "He's going to be okay, right?"

My mother pretends to be interested in Eva's window display. In the reflection in the glass, her face looks sad, but when she turns to me, she's all smiles. This is the same smile she wore when she told me that we were going to spend time in Last Chance this summer.

"We're hoping for the best!" Mom says a little too loudly. "He's got great doctors, and, well, the power of positive thinking, right?

Before I can answer, she sprints toward the Golden Palace.

Daisy seems relieved when Mom launches into restaurant mode, overseeing the dining room, giving orders in the kitchen. Lady Macbeth frowns when my mother explains that we have a "modified menu" today. Translation: Oma's not here and Daisy's too scared to prepare some of the more complicated dishes.

My mother has been giving Daisy tips to make the dishes look as good as they taste.

"Instead of piling the noodles, drape them with a slight swirl, then top them with sprigs of cilantro."

"A light crowning of crushed peanuts will brighten the glazed beef."

"Floating a few slivers of ginger in wonton soup makes it more inviting."

Recently, when Oma saw Daisy's garlic pork with gai lan, she said, "Thank you, Charlotte. Our dishes are looking better these days."

My mother almost fainted, but managed to sputter, "You're welcome, Mom. Anytime."

The sicker Opa gets, the nicer they are to each other. It means a lot to Oma that we are here. She may not say so, but like my grandfather taught me, watch the person, not the game. That's the tell. Sometimes when Mom's working at the Golden Palace, my grandmother puts her hands over her heart and lets out a soft sigh.

When I take a break and go home, I'm surprised to find Oma in Mom's room. She's just standing there, looking at some photos of my mother from when she was a kid.

"Oh, Maizy! You startled me. I was just here for this."

Oma grabs the closest thing to her—a scented candle shaped like an ice cream sundae.

"Do you want to talk a little bit, Oma? You're always so busy. I hardly see you."

My grandmother lowers herself into the beanbag chair. "A couple minutes. Then I need to check on that old goat downstairs."

I remember how lost Oma and Opa looked on the food commercial set all those years ago, but how at home they are here. "What was it like living in Last Chance most of your life?" I ask her.

"Your opa and I have had a great time here." Oma pauses. "It wasn't so easy for your mom, though. Being the only non-white kid in town."

"Did you ever want to move?"

Oma nods. "At times, yes. But it was my choice to stay in Last Chance. I could have gone back to Philadelphia, where I was from, and started a career. Before I met your grandfather, I wanted to be a math teacher. Once we were together, though, there was no question about what I'd do with my life."

"Because you love the restaurant business?"

"Because I love your grandfather," she says. "Now, speaking of that grumpy old man, Maizy, help me out of this beanbag so I can go down and see what trouble he's causing now."

I sit at the top of the stairs and listen to the comforting sound of the two of them talking. Young Oma must have really loved Opa to give up so much. I think about Lulu and about Opa's mother, Ana, and about my grandmother. All young Chinese American women who moved away from big cities to this small town to be with their husbands. And then there's my mom, who went in the opposite direction to follow her dream, or maybe to find it.

American Dream

1905

Lulu was right. They were Americans. "Home is where your heart is," she told Lucky. That their child would be raised here, in their adopted hometown of Last Chance, Minnesota—in the heartland of the United States—was an easy decision. Rebuilding the Golden Palace, however, was more difficult.

Even though Lucky dressed like a businessman in his finely tailored suit and spoke flawless English, banks refused to lend them the money they needed to rebuild. It didn't matter that the Golden Palace had been successful, or that he carried letters of introduction from the mayor, Sheriff Swain, and several prominent citizens. All that the white bankers could see was that Lucky was Chinese.

Finally, Lucky was forced to borrow from untrustworthy men. They charged high interest rates. And they made it clear that if the loans weren't repaid on time, they would harm Lucky's family.

When Lucky began rebuilding the Golden Palace, many locals pitched in to help. Everyone wanted to show their appreciation to the neighbors who had always been there for them. Now it was time for them to repay Lucky and Lulu.

At last, the Golden Palace was ready for its grand reopening. Lucky stood with Lulu, who was holding their baby. Mr. and Mrs. Philips were tickled when they found out the baby was named for them. They sent a chest full of baby clothes, toys, beddings, and blankets to Baby Philip.

Life was looking good for Lucky and his family.

Chapter 59

"Baby Philip, that was your father, right, Opa?"

Opa tries to smile, but looks tired. "Yes, my dad was named after a millionaire!"

I'll be sure to tell Emmy about this. She's including the Golden Palace in her graduate research paper and promises to visit.

Ever since Oma thanked her, Mom's been trying even harder to impress my grandmother with her food stylist skills. She always looks for a reaction before the dishes go out into the dining room. If Oma nods or gives a compliment, Mom can't hide her joy. Both are starting to thaw, but it's a slow process. Like icebergs, there's a lot below the surface.

"Maizy, please take those to Lady Macbeth." My mother gestures to a platter of ma po bean curd, bitter melon soup, and broccoli beef. The tray is heavy, but I can carry it with one hand.

Lady Macbeth looks down her nose at the meal in front of her. "I don't see my dry-fried string beans."

"I couldn't bring everything at once. I'm going back to get the rest now."

"Well, hurry!" She aims her chopsticks at me like a weapon. Logan says that ninjas can kill you by throwing a single chopstick. "You know I don't like cold food!"

And I don't like you, I think, but I keep it to myself.

Lady Macbeth lingers over her meal as the Noisy Family children toss fistfuls of noodles at each other. The mother tries to calm them down, while the father ignores the chaos.

I roll a fresh sheet of paper into the typewriter. It's more work to be mean than it is to be nice, I write for Lady Macbeth. Then I type four more fortunes. When I bring them to the Noisy Family, the oldest girl, Jodi, reads them out loud, stunning the younger siblings into silence.

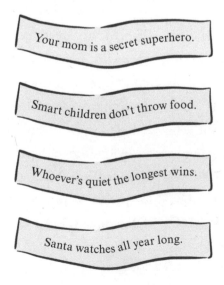

Your mom is a secret superhero.

Smart children don't throw food.

Whoever's quiet the longest wins.

Santa watches all year long.

Chapter 60

Lady Macbeth has been here almost three hours. We should charge her rent for taking up space.

"It's not so bad." Daisy is rooting through the garbage in search of recyclables. "It makes it look like we have customers." She holds up a plastic container. "One hundred percent of baby sea turtles have plastic in their tiny stomachs. They mistake floating garbage for food."

Lady Macbeth's fortune cookie sits unopened. At last she stands, abandoning the leftovers. Unasked, I pack them to go. Anger rises in my belly when she weaves her skinny figure around the tables toward the door. Opa is sick; Oma and my mom are upset; someone stole Bud, left a bigoted letter, and then painted a slur on him.

So much is happening, and all this selfish lady does is waste food, show off how rich she is, and wonder why her tea isn't hot. I slam her plates into the dirty-dish bin, working myself up—until I throw down the towel. I have a few things to say to Lady Macbeth. On my way out, I grab the to-go bag.

Erik is with Sidekick on Main Street. Instead of hiding, I

keep walking. I look for a reaction when he sees the paint on my fishing vest, but his face is blank.

Lady Macbeth couldn't have gotten far. Recently, she's started using a cane, probably so she can whack people with it. With each step I take, I calm down a little more. Eventually I talk myself out of confronting her. I'm already practically at her house. Maybe I'll just leave the leftovers on her front porch, ring the doorbell, and run.

From behind the overgrown weeds in her front yard, I wait until Lady Macbeth closes the door. It makes sense that she lives in the creepy mansion that gave me the chills when I first got to Last Chance. I tiptoe up the porch stairs, put the to-go bag down, and start to leave when I hear something. A whisper?

The heavy wooden door isn't closed all the way. I poke my head in, bracing myself for whatever scary surprises there might be.

I'm shocked.

Instead of broken furniture, cobwebs, and skeletons, I see beauty. Though I know I shouldn't, I take a step inside the house. My eyes widen. Is this how Lucky felt the first time he saw the Philips Mansion? Intricate wood panels line the walls and a huge crystal chandelier hangs overhead, casting twinkling rainbows all around me.

I hear a piano playing. My curiosity draws me deeper inside and I find myself in a room filled floor to ceiling with books. I'm awestruck, like Belle the first time she sees Beast's library. I half expect Beast to show up.

"Intruder! Intruder, stop!" someone cries.

Chapter 61

whirl around. The music has stopped. Lady Macbeth is holding up her cane, ready to strike.

"Sorry!" I try not to sound scared. "Your door was open?"

"That doesn't give you license to come in!" Lady Macbeth points a gnarled finger at an overstuffed chair in the next room. "Sit."

We're not at the Golden Palace, but I do as I'm told.

"Now then." Lady Macbeth perches on the red velvet couch across from me. Her posture is impeccable. "Speak, Maizy. You seem like a girl who has a lot to say."

I'm surprised she knows my name.

"Cat got your tongue?" A smug smile forms on her thin lips.

She doesn't scare me! Well, not too much.

"I brought your leftovers. You order too much food!" As soon as the words leave my mouth, I realize how stupid I sound. I broke into someone's house because they order a lot of food? I add weakly, "Plus, you have a bad attitude?"

Lady Macbeth's face contorts. The smirk leads to a smile,

then a laugh that won't stop. "Oh, Maizy." Lady Macbeth sounds like she's talking to a small child. "You don't have any idea why I order so much, do you?"

"Showing off your money?"

She shakes her head.

"Can't choose just one dish?" I try.

I look around. There are photos and paintings everywhere. Lady Macbeth as a little girl, Lady Macbeth as a debutante, Lady Macbeth on her wedding day with a handsome young groom.

She follows my gaze. "My husband, Leonard." My eyes go to a photo of her with Leonard and a little boy. "Our only child," Lady Macbeth explains.

"Where is he now?" I'll bet she was so mean she drove him away.

"Emmett died when he was a toddler. Scarlet fever. My husband passed away months later from the same illness . . . and from a broken heart."

My mouth opens, but nothing comes out.

Lady Macbeth returns to a lighter subject. "Your question about the food? Maybe you haven't noticed, but the Golden Palace isn't doing well. The fewer the customers, the more I order." When I look confused, she adds, "To help keep the restaurant in business."

Her watery blue eyes are trained on me.

"But . . . why . . . then . . . oh." My words, my thoughts are all tossed together like a plate of chop suey.

"Don't you dare tell anyone," Lady Macbeth warns. Her

voice is stern, but her face has a rosy flush I hadn't noticed before. "If you do, I'll deny it. Your grandparents would never ask for help. They're used to being the ones to help others, like giving food and jobs to relatives and friends." She leans in and whispers, "Like Daisy."

"Daisy?" I'm surprised to hear her name in this conversation.

Lady Macbeth rearranges her pearl necklace. "When that girl first landed in Last Chance, she didn't know a soul. Your grandmother got her a job at the bank and library. After the building flooded and closed, Daisy came to work at the Golden Palace. Anyone with half a brain knows that the restaurant doesn't need another person on payroll."

That's when it hits me hard. Lady Macbeth isn't the enemy, and like a paper son, Daisy needed help.

Lady Macbeth doesn't sit in the middle of the restaurant so that everyone can see her—she sits in the middle so she can see everyone. Imagine having to come home to this big, empty house.

Opa's mother told him, "Things aren't always what they seem. The same goes for people."

How could I have been so wrong about Lady Macbeth? Who else have I been wrong about?

Chapter 62

O pa's been quiet lately. It's an effort for him to just aim the television remote. This time, when he presses a button, instead of the volume going up, the hospital bed that Mom ordered threatens to fold him in half.

"Help!"

I lunge for the emergency stop, and when Opa's comfortable again, I turn up the television sound for him. He's enjoying watching Carlos! work his way through a seafood buffet in Cape Cod.

There's a knock on the door. On his way to worming, Logan drops off the August issue of *Minnesota Dontcha Know*, the one with Mayor Whitlock's article about Bud.

"Opa." I hold up the magazine. "It's here!"

Bigotry and the Bear

Opinion

By Jefferson P. Whitlock

Bud the Bear is a fixture in the tiny Minnesota town of Last Chance, population 4,428. The hand-carved wooden statue stands seven feet tall and first appeared over a hundred years ago when Chinese immigrant Lucky Chen took over the Golden Grille, now known as the Golden Palace. Generations have been welcomed into the Chen family's Chinese restaurant by "Bud," who's become a symbol of the town. For years, visitors have had their photos taken with this famous bear.

However, not everyone is a fan of Bud. One night last month the statue disappeared, and in its place was a racially tinged ransom note. (Because *Minnesota Dontcha Know* is a family magazine, we will not be publishing the note.) The handwritten missive clearly targeted the Chen family, the only Chinese in the area. In addition to stereotypical mocking language, it referenced racist images and demanded 1,000 yen (which is Japanese currency) for the return of Bud the Bear, and ended with "Go home to China!"

Bud's owners, and the proprietors of the Golden Palace, John and Lydia Chen, declined to talk to us, but their eleven-year-old granddaughter, Maizy Chen, of Los Angeles, who is visiting Last Chance, observed, "It's bad enough they took Bud, but the note was clearly meant to harm. It was a racist and hateful message."

The note was unsigned, and for many weeks Bud remained missing. The county sheriff's office attributed Bud's disappearance and the note to "just some kids doing a prank."

Last Chance school principal Glenn Holmes said, "I have long hoped that our area would be welcoming to all. Unfortunately, there are some who seek to taunt those who are not like themselves."

Townsperson Dorrie Hurley weighed in, saying, "I'm the least prejudiced person in the world. I'll miss the bear, but people are too sensitive. Freedom of speech is in the Constitution." But in the words of dairy farmer Mary Peterson, "There is no room here for this sort of thing."

After weeks of being unaccounted for, Bud the Bear was found deep in the woods by Finnigan "Finn" Olson, age eight. Townsfolk united to return the bear to the Golden Palace, where he now stands. The kidnappers were never identified, but recently, bigotry struck again, this time in the form of graffiti. Bud the Bear was attacked with a paintbrush when someone painted a derogatory statement on him.

There has been a lot in the news about tolerance and/or the lack of it. Last Chance is a friendly town. Yet prejudice still hides in the shadows. Perhaps Maizy put it best when she said, "Isn't it time that we've evolved past prejudice?"

For now, beloved Bud the Bear is home in front of the Golden Palace, free of hateful messages. However, the perpetrator is still among us. Let's hope that Last Chance can move forward and show the world that we can all get along.

Chapter 63

Mayor Whitlock made lots of great points. If tiny Last Chance has issues with prejudice, is it any wonder that entire countries can't get along?

"Was it hard growing up here?" Mom and I are folding laundry on the bed. I'm in charge of Opa's handkerchiefs.

"Sometimes, yes." She's looking at a pair of mismatched socks. "Why do you ask?"

"Oma mentioned that it might not have been easy for you."

Mom stops sorting laundry. "I didn't think she ever noticed."

"Are you kidding? Oma notices everything!"

Mom laughs. "I guess you're right about that. I've always craved excitement. I wanted to live somewhere where I could reinvent myself—a place I could fit in. Here, my claim to fame was that I was the daughter of the Chinese restaurant owners. That's not what I wanted to be known as."

"What did you want to be known as?"

My mother pauses. "To be my own person, I guess. To make my own way and not just do what was expected of me."

"What did Oma and Opa say about that?" Mom and I talk about so much stuff, but I never thought to ask about her childhood before.

"Nothing. They never said anything. Oh, sometimes Opa would launch into a story about how hard it was for his grandfather, but to me that was ancient history. And all Oma cared about was the Golden Palace."

That's not true, I want to tell her.

"You know," I say, "Oma told me that at one time she wanted to be a math teacher." Opa's handkerchiefs are now stacked in an orderly pile.

Mom stops folding a shirt. "She told you that?"

"You should talk to her. I think there's a lot you both don't know about each other."

Chapter 64

At the Golden Palace, Mayor Whitlock is greeted like a hero. Everyone loved his article. Even Lady Macbeth. Oma makes sure his lunch is on the house, and Daisy asks him to sign her *Dontcha Know*, which delights him. He offers to sign a copy for me, too.

I'm a bit of a celebrity. Logan is totally impressed with my interview. Mom, Oma, and Opa can't stop talking about it. Principal Holmes says that my quote *Isn't it time that we've evolved past prejudice?* is classic.

There's only one problem.

I never said that.

"Maizy Chen!" Mayor Whitlock waves his chopsticks in the air like an orchestra conductor. "Well, what did you think?"

"I thought it was great."

"My editor thought so, too. We've gotten record numbers of online hits, so they're going to feature the article all month!"

He's in such a great mood, I don't want to ruin it. Still,

there's something that's been bothering me. I clear my throat.

"I didn't say that stuff about evolving past prejudice."

"Technically, you may not have." He studies the menu. "But I paraphrased what you had been saying—in the spirit of the interview, of course."

When I don't respond, Mayor Whitlock puts the menu down. "Maizy, you did say it. Maybe not those specific words, but it's what you meant. That was a powerful statement. Maybe even the crux of the story. Let's just let people think you said it."

I nod.

But I don't feel good about this.

Chapter 65

The days are slowing down. Werner gets up to leave. He looks exhausted. Opa wasn't talking much today, so Werner kept up the chatter with Carlos! about baked potato toppings.

I walk him out and stop at the mailbox. It's all bills, bills, bills, or as Oma says, "Those darn bills!"

Wait! The last envelope is from Carlos! I rip it open. On crisp white stationery is . . . a form letter.

Dear Restaurant Owner:

Thank you for your interest in Carlos! We have reviewed your inquiry about <u>Golden Palace</u>, and though your restaurant is certainly unique, our schedule is full for the next year.

Keep watching Carlos! and thank you for your support!

Sincerely,
Bobbie Cannon
Intern, Carlos! Enterprises

My heart sinks. I'm about to crumple the paper when I notice something on the back.

Dear Maizy!

I love what you wrote about your grandparents' restaurant! Such an amazing history! I'll bet the food is great, too. Please tell your grandfather that I'm rooting for him to get well soon and that if I am ever in the area, I will be sure to visit the Golden Palace!

All best,
Carlos!

I rush into the house. Opa is napping in the hospital bed. Mom no longer takes him to the doctor. Now the doctor comes here.

I let Opa sleep. It's Delish Dish Week, which means reruns of Carlos! 24/7. Opa and I don't mind. Our favorite is the one where Carlos! visits Dining Dark in Spruce Pine, North Carolina. That's where "you eat with the lights off and with your hands to heighten the culinary experience!"

We tried eating in the dark after we watched the show the first time. Not only was Opa able to identify the dishes and their ingredients, he could tell if Oma or Daisy cooked it.

After about an hour, Opa begins to stir.

"Opa? Opa, you up?"

His eyes flutter open. "Charlotte? Why aren't you in school?"

"It's me, Maizy. Carlos! wants you to get well soon!"

Opa looks around. "Carlos! is here?"

I adjust the bed for him. "No, Opa." I show him the letter. "He wrote to us."

I read the letter out loud, then hand it over.

Opa's face lights up.

I can't begin to describe how much I love my grandfather. Even though he's right here, I miss him already. I start to tear up.

"Oh, Maizy." Opa clasps his hands around mine to stop them from shaking. "Don't waste any tears on a sick old man!"

I let out a groan and pull away. "Why do you say things like that? It's not funny. Opa, it's mean."

He produces a fresh handkerchief from his sleeve and hands it to me. "That's why I do it." My grandfather's thin shoulders bounce up and down as he chuckles. His pajamas look three sizes too big.

"You do it because it's mean?"

Opa is not making sense. The excitement from Carlos! has probably rattled him. He gets confused.

The mischievous look that's been missing from his face for a long time is back. "Your oma and mother are so sad, it depresses me. They think I can't see them, but I do. They act like they're at my funeral. But when I tell them I'm going to die soon, they get angry."

What kind of weird logic is that?

Wait! He's playing them like a hand of poker. "You'd rather have people mad at you than be sad because of you. You're making them mad on purpose!"

"You're a smart cookie, Maizy Chen!"

Opa motions for me to help him adjust his pillow. When he turns his attention back to Carlos!, I hold back tears. I don't want to be mad or sad, but right now I'm both.

Opa and I don't talk about what's happening. Instead, we try to make each other feel better by laughing louder at jokes, and smiling a lot. Just wait until he finds out about my paper sons research. So far more than a dozen people have replied to Emmy's post about Last Chance paper sons. Most want to know about Lucky and the Golden Palace, but besides Lynn Fong in New Jersey, there are a few possible paper son descendants who have also been in touch.

Opa is too excited about the letter to nap. "Why don't you tell me about Lucky?" I ask. "I'll bet Carlos! would have loved to meet him."

Earthquake

1906

No one was prepared when the ground started shaking. The rumble turned into a roar. People were tossed from their beds.

Thousands died. Most of the city was destroyed, and more than half the population was homeless. The headlines shouted, *EARTHQUAKE AND FIRE: SAN FRANCISCO IN RUINS.*

Though Lucky and Lulu were two thousand miles away, they worried about their friends in San Francisco. The earthquake's silver lining was that all the birth records in San Francisco had been destroyed. This paved the way for paper sons to come to America. Now there was no way to confirm who was born in the United States or who had immigrated.

By then, many Chinese had passed along stories about a restaurant in the middle of America that was an oasis of safety, friendship, and home-cooked meals. Lucky and Lulu's son, Philip, grew up with a revolving door of "uncles" and "cousins," and the wall of photos grew in the back office.

Philip graduated with honors from high school and in 1921 earned a scholarship to St. Ignatius College in San Francisco. On a sunny afternoon, he said goodbye to his parents and Bud the Bear, then boarded the train.

It only took a few months for Philip to grow homesick. The big city wasn't for him.

Lucky and Lulu were happy to have their son home, but disappointed that he didn't return with a bride. There weren't any marriage prospects for him in Last Chance. In many states, it was against the law for a Chinese person to marry outside their race. And though it wasn't illegal in Minnesota, no white family would have accepted their daughter marrying a Chinese man, even if he was an American. Eventually, Lulu wrote to friends back in San Francisco. In those days, arranged marriages weren't uncommon.

Though shy in each other's company at first, Philip and his new wife, Ana, learned to love each other. She was quite a firecracker and loved Last Chance, despite having come from a big city. The young couple even added their own touches to the Golden Palace, like colorful paper lanterns. In time, they had a son. They named him after the minister who married them— John Robert, though everyone called him Johnny.

Chapter 66

"Johnny? That's you, right, Opa? You're Johnny!"

The Lucky Stories had been just that, stories. But now they're becoming real. There's Bud, and the photo of bride Lulu in a silver frame.

I look up the San Francisco earthquake. One of the newspaper headlines from 1906 reads:

3000 DEAD; $300,000,000 LOST
SAN FRANCISCO IS OBLITERATED

Is this what Lucky saw, too? So much was destroyed. But Opa had said there was a silver lining. When I wrote Emmy about it, she replied:

> The earthquake opened the door for more Chinese immigrants to come to America. Still, it wasn't easy. For European immigrants, processing could be done

within hours. Yet, for the Chinese, coming through Angel Island in San Francisco or Ellis Island in New York could last weeks, months, and in some cases as long as two years. These immigrants stayed in custody until they were released–or were sent back to China.

Chapter 67

Riley and her grandparents are at the restaurant for dinner. Logan says she lives with them. When she introduces me as "my friend Maizy," the tray I'm carrying suddenly feels lighter.

After their meal, Riley pulls me aside. "I don't know if this is anything, but Caroline said her brother Erik came home really late the night that Bud went missing. He'd been drinking with his friends and they do really dumb things when they're drunk. And the next morning, he joked that he saw a bear in the woods."

With this information, I got dealt a promising new card. Now that Bud's home, I've eased up on tracking down the culprits. But knowing this about Erik changes the game.

I'm clearing their table when Principal Holmes takes a seat. He's got on a *There Their They're* T-shirt.

"Can we talk?" I begin. Principal Holmes looks curious when I sit down. I have to be quick in case Mom shows up. "You have my permission to date my mother."

I'm expecting a huge "thank you," but instead, he strokes

his chin as he studies the tea leaves floating at the top of his cup.

Did I just say something stupid?

"Maizy, your mother and I have pledged never to lose touch again. I love her, but not in that way. My heart belongs to someone else."

"WHAT?" I lower my voice. "Excuse me?"

Mom and Principal Holmes are always happy around each other. They went to prom together. They share secrets. They held hands!

Lady Macbeth is watching.

How could I have misjudged this so badly? I'm stunned, not to mention humiliated. Has he been leading her on all this time?

"Does my mother know about this other person?"

"Chris," Principal Holmes says, nodding. "She does, and she approves."

"So Chris is your girlfriend?" My voice is flat.

"No . . . not girlfriend."

"Your wife?"

He shakes his head. "Chris is my husband," Principal Holmes corrects me. "We're practically newlyweds! I'm trying to talk him into moving to Last Chance, but for now we're mostly in Minneapolis, where he works."

Lady Macbeth returns to her eggplant. The purple matches her dress.

"How come you don't wear a ring?"

"Partly because we haven't found the perfect ones yet,

and also because not everyone around here is happy that we got married."

"I don't understand why you're trying to make the bigots feel comfortable," I say as I refill his teacup.

There's a loud whoop at the next table. When I glance over, Lady Macbeth is dabbing her mouth with a napkin.

Principal Holmes nods slowly. "Maizy, you have an excellent point. That's what Chris keeps saying, too."

After he gives me his order, Lady Macbeth motions me over and whispers, "Put his meal on my bill. A wedding present."

I head to the kitchen, where I spy Oma lingering around Daisy's tip jar. She pulls out ten dollars from her pocket and stuffs it inside. Lady Macbeth and Oma have a lot in common. Neither is as crusty as they want you to believe.

When Principal Holmes is done with his meal, instead of a check, I hand him a Golden Palace to-go box. On a bed of uncooked rice, there are fortune cookies that say things like:

Chris and Glenn, now and forever . . .

May you live happily ever after!

Put a ring on it.

Chapter 68

The magazine article has brought in some new business, mostly people from other towns. Many customers go out of their way to let us know they aren't racist by saying things like "It's a shame what happened." And "You people are so brave." One lady tells me, "You're so cute, just like a doll."

Everyone has their photo taken with Bud.

Mayor Whitlock is reading the newspaper. He doesn't look up when I stand by his table.

"I know who took Bud and wrote on him." Now I have his full attention. "Erik Fisk and his friends."

Mayor Whitlock looks shocked. "Do you have proof?"

"Erik was out drinking the night Bud went missing. There was an empty whiskey bottle near where Bud was found. That night Bud got written on, Erik and his friends were out drinking whiskey again."

He nods. "It sounds like there's something there, but it's circumstantial evidence."

"Circumstantial?"

"That means it's not one hundred percent certain that Erik and his friends did it." Mayor Whitlock gets serious. "I'll look into this. But until we know for sure, please don't mention it to anyone."

I feel a sense of relief knowing that maybe now justice will be served.

Back at home, Carlos! is in a pizzeria. When he tosses the dough, it lands on his head. I laugh and wait for Opa to join me, but he looks distracted. His mind has been wandering a lot these days. Maybe I can get him to tell me another story. When he talks about Lucky, my grandfather remembers every detail.

"What was that?" Opa asks.

"Another Lucky Story?" I ask again. "Can you tell me one?"

Opa shuts his eyes, and I'm afraid he's too tired. But when he opens them, I can tell he's game.

"I guess I can manage another story for my favorite grandchild," he says. "Shall we begin?"

One Hundred Years

1941

Eventually, Philip and Ana took over the restaurant. Still, Lucky and Lulu showed up every day, rubbed Bud the Bear's paw for good luck, and held court at a table near the kitchen. They loved helping take care of young Johnny, who had the run of the restaurant.

Business was booming. Famous author F. Scott Fitzgerald even stopped by the Golden Palace on his way to visit his hometown of Saint Paul. He pronounced his meal "jolly good."

However, the good days were not to last.

To the shock of the world, newspaper headlines shouted: *WAR! Pearl Harbor Bombed by Japanese Planes*

Suddenly Lucky and his family became suspect. Though they were not Japanese, to many they looked like they could be. Most of Johnny's classmates, except for a German immigrant named Warner Werner, accused him of being a spy.

Lulu insisted that her grandson always had a note pinned to his jacket that read *I am a Chinese American* so he would be less of a target. Lucky hung a huge *We Are American* sign outside the Golden Palace.

When someone crossed it out and wrote *GO HOME!* Johnny was confused. "But we are home, aren't we?"

Business was bad. Many who had hid their prejudice now felt free to flaunt it. Determined to prove his allegiance to America, Philip enlisted to fight in World War II. Lucky wanted to go, too, but the United States military didn't take eighty-eight-year-old men.

By the time World War II ended, it had taken its toll on the entire country, and there was still resentment toward anyone who looked Asian.

Through it all, the Golden Palace served Last Chance. One day, after lunch hour, Lulu felt faint. When she reached for a chair to steady herself, she fell and hit her head. Lucky ran over to her.

Within minutes, Philip was driving his elderly parents to the hospital. "We don't take your kind," they were told when they arrived.

"It's because we're Chinese," Philip said angrily. "I am an American war veteran!"

"Not now," Lucky said from the back seat as he cradled Lulu in his arms. "Keep driving."

It took over an hour to get to the next hospital. The nurse took one look at Lulu and rushed her inside. A team of emergency doctors were called, but by then it was too late.

For Lucky, the Golden Palace was never the same without Lulu. Years later, when Lucky reached his hundredth birthday, the mayor of Last Chance presented him with the key to the city. Family, friends, and fans cheered. "Speech! Speech!"

Lucky was silent for so long that many thought his memory was failing him. But it was the opposite. Lucky was remembering growing up poor in China and his journey to an unknown land. He was remembering his best friend, Li Wei, and the men who ran him out of San Francisco. He was remembering Mr. and Mrs. Philips, Happy, and the paper sons who found their way to Last Chance. But most of all he remembered Lulu and the Golden Palace and his family.

Finally, he spoke. "I may have been born in China, but my life, my loves, and my home is here in Last Chance, Minnesota. Thank you to all who have been on this journey with me. Because of you, my heart is full."

Two days later, on August 27, 1953, Lucky Chen passed away.

Chapter 69

My heart.

"Opa, I am so sad that Lucky's Story is over."

His voice is shaky. "Over? Who said anything about it being over? Lucky coming to America and building the Golden Palace was just the beginning. Your great-great-grandfather grew to know and love Last Chance in a way few had. He didn't see it as a dusty little town in the middle of nowhere. Lucky saw promise and the future."

"The 'I am a Chinese American' note in the office," I say. "Was that the one you wore?"

"The very one! The day World War Two ended, I thought that the Golden Palace would immediately fill up again and that kids would stop taunting me." Opa pauses. "But I was wrong."

I want to ask him more, but he seems so tired.

"Maizy, bring that typewriter of yours back home," he orders. "There's something I want you to type up for me."

Before I can ask him what it is, Opa is sleeping.

Werner comes in with the dancing-pigs snow globe. He

sets it down near Opa. Then he whispers so as not to wake him, "My daughter, Kaitlyn, is having a baby!"

This is the happiest I've seen Werner in weeks.

I'm in the office swapping out fortunes when I overhear Mom and Oma.

"I don't know what I'd do without him," my grandmother says.

My mother is making radish roses. "Oh, Mom," she says, handing my grandmother a flower. "You'll always have the Golden Palace."

"This restaurant was his dream, not mine," Oma says softly.

"Will you tell me about your dream?" my mother asks.

My grandmother brushes off some cilantro from Mom's shirt. "My dream came true. It was to spend my life with your father—and have a daughter." She pauses. "Charlotte, I used to think that when you left Last Chance, you wanted to get away from me and Opa. But that's not what it was, was it? Now I realize you were trying to get closer to your own dream, not live mine. Your father always hoped that you'd take over the Golden Palace—but I secretly hoped you wouldn't."

Mom looks shocked. "I thought that's what you wanted me to do and why you were mad at me. . . ."

Oma picks up a paring knife and, copying my mom, starts making radish roses. "Charlotte, you've had so many freedoms in your lifetime. Ones that I would have never attempted by myself. You are fearless. You moved to a big city. You have a successful career, you bought a house, and you had a beautiful daughter on your own. . . ."

"You and Dad made your life here at the Golden Palace," Mom tells her. "I'm proud of that. I want to honor my legacy—but in my own way."

When Oma walks away without speaking, Mom looks crushed.

I step aside so my grandmother can take something out of a cabinet. It's a *Food Stylists Monthly* magazine. One with my mother on the cover.

"It took me a while to come around." Oma shows her the magazine. "I've subscribed to this for years. I look for you in every issue. I'm so proud of you, Charlotte."

The silence is only broken when my mother begins to cry.

When Principal Holmes mended Bud's broken paw, he said it was "stronger than ever."

I hope that it will be that way for Mom and Oma, too.

Chapter 70

Opa is not himself. The doctor has been to the house twice this week and it's only Wednesday. Oma is home all the time. Mom keeps asking if I want to talk about what's happening. After months of wondering, now I don't want to know. Only Opa remains upbeat, but it's an effort for him.

When I tell my grandfather about my paper sons research, he's thrilled. Opa's even able to fill me in about Eddie Fong and some of the others, including one man who went to work for NASA, and another who invented a new type of tomato.

"I thought I'd be done by now," I apologize. "But it's taking so long."

Opa motions me closer. I have to listen hard to make out what he's saying. "Of course it's taking a long time . . . looking back at several lifetimes. . . . Gather the stories. . . . Don't lose sight of what Lucky and the paper sons have in common."

I nod. "The Golden Palace and Last Chance."

My grandfather struggles to speak. "You, Maizy. You're the connection. They all have you in common."

Before I can ask him what he means, Opa is asleep.

Chapter 71

I'm thinking back to the day we first drove up to the Golden Palace, and the people I met, like Lady Macbeth and Logan and Daisy. Then there was Bud's kidnapping and Mayor Whitlock's article. But the more I reminisce, the more something seems off. Things aren't adding up. That's when it hits me. Like in poker, this is a fouled deck.

There are three empty mugs lined up in front of Logan. He motions for a fourth.

"You've had enough root beer floats for one day." Eva has seen this before. We all know how Logan gets when he's had too much sugar.

"Yeah, but I got worm money!" Logan pats his pocket. "Did really well today."

"Just don't bring them in here. Remember what happened last time."

I'm sweaty from running all over town looking for Logan. Eva sets an icy lemonade in front of me. I wait until she leaves, then say, "Logan, the writing on Bud . . . I know who did it!"

"Who?!"

I try to catch my breath. My head is spinning.

"Mayor Whitlock told me that *Minnesota Dontcha Know* articles have to be submitted at least two weeks before the new month." Logan motions for me to talk faster. "His article included the horrible stuff painted on Bud—but that happened AFTER he turned in his article."

"Wait, what?" Logan's eyes widen.

"I'm not sure if Mayor Whitlock had a part in Bud's kidnapping. But how could he have known that someone was going to paint Bud?"

Logan sees where I'm going with this. "He had to have been in on it! But why would he do that?"

In poker, I can observe the cards in front of me. This is a different game, but I see what Mayor Whitlock was up to.

"Double barrel," I explain. "That's when your poker hand isn't that strong, so you double down. You try to fool your opponents into thinking you have something big. Mayor Whitlock added the graffiti to the article to give it more of a punch."

"You're sure he didn't change the article after he submitted it?" Logan presses.

"I'm ninety-nine-point-nine percent sure."

"Maizy, for something this big, you need to be one hundred percent."

Logan's right. Circumstantial evidence is not enough. If Mayor Whitlock cheated, I need confirmation. I'm hoping that, like Opa has said about poker, "eventually all the cards will be revealed."

Mayor Whitlock welcomes me into his office with a broad smile. He's framed the article and hung it on the wall. "My editor is nominating me for the J. Daniels Award," he says. "To win it twice could make a person famous."

My heart is racing, but my poker face is solid.

"What can I do for you, Maizy?"

"I was wondering . . ." I begin setting the trap, like Opa taught me in poker. "If I were to submit something to *Dontcha Know*, could I get it into next month's issue?"

"Like a little story?"

I nod. "Something like that."

Though he's at home in bed, I can hear Opa instructing me, "You need to know your position. That means the order people play." But in this case, it's the order and dates articles are submitted.

"Sorry, Maizy, you've missed the deadline. Remember the magazine needs at least two weeks' lead time. Nothing can be added or changed because it's printed in Iowa and then shipped all over Minnesota."

"What if the story is really good?" I ask.

In poker, it's best to go last so you can see what cards everyone else is playing.

"No exceptions," Mayor Whitlock says firmly. "Once the press is rolling, that's it."

"Okay, thanks anyway."

A weight has been lifted, but I feel crushed at the same time. I thought Mayor Whitlock and I were on the same side. He's smiling and waving as I leave. Just because someone is friendly doesn't mean they're your friend.

With my poker face in play, I wave back. I don't show him my cards yet. I should probably tell Mom or my grandparents first. If Mayor Whitlock knew ahead of time that Erik or someone else was going to paint on Bud, he could have stopped a hate crime. But if Mayor Whitlock did it himself and is lying about it, that's even worse. And either way, he used race and hatred to put my family down and raise himself up.

I'm close to the house. There's a crowd outside. An ambulance is in the driveway with red lights blinking.

"Oh no. No, no, no!"

Werner is sitting on the curb with his head in his hands. Mom and Oma are clutching each other.

"Opa! Is Opa okay?" I shout as I run toward them.

Oma looks right at me. She opens her mouth, but no sound comes out.

Mom gathers me in her arms.

Chapter 72

Unless you count when I was born, I've never been to a hospital before. The lights are bright and the room smells like a bad imitation of the woods. In Opa's room, Mom and Oma hold hands, looking grim as sorrow wraps them closer together.

Opa's hospital bed here is way fancier than the one he has at home. A TV is mounted to the wall with a soap opera on mute. I change the channel to Carlos! Tubes are attached to my grandfather's thin arms. A machine monitors his heart with squiggly lines. It reminds me of the Richter scale we learned about in school when studying earthquakes.

"The food here is terrible." Opa's voice is less than a whisper. Each word is an effort. "If it doesn't kill you, nothing will!"

I fake a laugh. Every part of me hurts. I put on my poker face and hope that no one can see past it.

"Opa, you have to get well. Otherwise, who will tell stories about Lucky and the Golden Palace?"

Before he can respond, a nurse opens the door. Her scrubs

have silly dancing teddy bears on them, and for a moment they distract me from the sadness. "Visiting hours are over." She sounds apologetic.

Mom helps Oma out of the room. I'm in the hallway when something tells me to turn around. Opa struggles to sit up. He looks weak, but I see a familiar spark in his eyes. "Maizy, I'm betting on you to tell our stories," I hear him say.

Then the door closes.

Chapter 73

Friends and neighbors bring condolences that go unheard and casseroles that go untouched. My grandmother hasn't been to the Golden Palace since Opa passed away. My mother doesn't stop crying, even though she's run out of tears. I haven't cried at all. The only time I take off my poker face is when I'm alone. But even then I don't cry. There must be something wrong with me.

Chapter 74

The church doors open to a steady flow of people. It looks like the entire town of Last Chance, Minnesota, is here. I've never been to a funeral before. So many firsts. Eva is already seated. She's wearing a dark dress and a heartbroken look on her face.

I have a dress on, too. A blue one I dug out of Mom's closet. When Oma saw me wearing Opa's fishing vest over it, I was afraid she might not approve. Instead, she hugged me.

Principal Holmes is with Mom. A tall man wearing a tan suit stands nearby, looking uncomfortable. My mother gives him a warm smile and admires his and Principal Holmes's matching wedding rings.

Lady Beth has entered the church. Even with her cane, she can barely walk. News of my grandfather's death has hit her hard. Lady Beth looks so frail, like a baby bird. Daisy's been delivering food to her house and stays to make sure she eats.

Principal Holmes takes Lady Beth's arm and helps her to

her seat, sitting down next to her. Chris is on her other side. Together they hold her up.

Daisy is standing against the wall, biting her fingernails. Her eyes and nose are red. She needs someone to tell her what to do. Oma motions her toward the front pew. "You will sit with the family."

Logan arrives with his parents. He's wearing a crisp white shirt. His red tie is too long, and his navy pants are too short.

"Are you mad at me, Maizy? Did I do something wrong?"

I shake my head. It's the opposite. That's why I haven't wanted to see him all week. Logan makes me think of Last Chance, and my grandparents, and the Golden Palace. I don't want to keep saying goodbye.

Riley is here. Her grandparents are talking to Oma. They have their heads bowed like a football huddle. I'm glad the Mean Girls aren't around. I don't see Werner.

"Maizy," Riley says, "I'm so sorry about your grandpa. I don't know what I'd do if anything happened to Bomma or Bompa. If you ever want to talk, I'm here."

I nod and she squeezes my hands. "You probably want to be with your relatives," she says.

"My relatives?"

There's a group of Chinese people I don't recognize. All of them are looking at me.

"Maizy?" A woman approaches. Her two young children hang back with their father. "I'm Lynn Fong from New Jersey. I heard about your grandfather's passing from Emmy Tsai."

"Lynn Fong," I say, stunned.

We emailed, but she was just a name. Now here she is, a real person. Total strangers traveled across the country to bid farewell to Opa?

"I'm so sorry for your loss," Ms. Fong is telling me. Her toddlers are crawling under the pews as their father attempts to catch them. "Ever since I was little, I've heard the most amazing stories about the Golden Palace. When your grandfather was just a boy, my grandfather taught him how to play cards. I've always wanted to visit. I wish I hadn't waited so long."

I look around and see more Chinese people, all different ages. They seek each other out, shaking hands, nodding, and talking in respectful tones. A young Asian woman approaches.

"Maizy, I'm Emmy Tsai from St. Catherine University in Saint Paul."

"Emmy?!" We've never met in person, but I feel like I know her.

I had sent Opa's online obituary to Emmy, and she asked if she could share it. I said yes, not realizing who might see it.

I search out Oma and Mom. My words are rushed as I tell them about the photos, and Emmy, and the Lucky Stories, and my paper sons research. When it dawns on Oma who these people are, she greets them like long-lost relatives.

I'm feeling better—until I spy Mayor Whitlock.

"Mrs. Chen!" Mayor Whitlock joins us. "As mayor of the

town and a longtime patron of the Golden Palace, I'd like to say a few words about your husband during the service, with your permission, of course."

Oma starts to thank him, when I interrupt.

"No."

Chapter 75

Mayor Whitlock ignores me. He's waiting for an answer from Oma. I scrutinize his tell—confident, self-important, pretentious.

"No." I raise my voice. "No, you may not speak at my grandfather's funeral. And you are not welcome at the Golden Palace ever again."

I step between him and Oma, forcing him to look at me. "Dontcha want to know why?" He may be older than me, and bigger than me, but I hold all the cards.

Mayor Whitlock stands taller, but I don't flinch. Without taking my eyes off him, I touch the paint on my fishing vest. "I know" is all I say.

That's when he folds and walks away.

"Maizy?" my grandmother asks.

"I'll explain later, Oma."

Today is not about Mayor Whitlock. Today is about my grandfather. Mom and I guide Oma to the front pew and join Daisy. I look around the church. It's a full house. Opa would have loved that.

Chapter 76

At the end of the funeral service, the minister reads an invitation from Oma. "'Please join our family at the Golden Palace for a celebration of life.'"

Everyone rises to let us leave the church first, then follows. We parade down Main Street. When we get to the restaurant, Lazy Dog, who's been waiting with Bud, stands at attention.

Inside, Oma sinks into a chair. Other than when she pays the bills or takes a quick meal break, I've never seen her sitting down at the Golden Palace before.

People line up to ask, "Are you hungry?"

"Can I get you anything?"

"Would you like some hot tea?"

Daisy slipped out of the funeral service early to get back to the kitchen. She has poured all that Oma has taught her into this one afternoon.

"I've never seen so much food in my life," I tell her. "This is incredible."

"I know," Daisy says, bursting into tears of sorrow and exhaustion.

Werner comes over and gives me a bear hug.

Daisy blows her nose into a towel. "Werner and I did this together."

"Thank you. Both of you. Thank you." I try not to choke up. Everyone is being so nice that it's overwhelming.

Buffet tables are heavy with the Golden Palace specialties. Rows of fluffy char siu bao are alongside ones Werner made with Opa's favorite bratwurst fillings.

Principal Holmes and Chris have not left Lady Beth's side. I slip her a cookie. Principal Holmes reads the fortune to her: "'Your kind heart is appreciated.'"

Lady Beth's eyes meet mine. Where I once saw meanness, I now see compassion.

Finn wasn't at the funeral, but he's come into the restaurant.

"Have some food," I tell him.

"I'm not hungry. I just wanted to see your grandma."

He goes up to Oma and hugs her for a long time. "I'm sorry you're sad," he says before leaving.

Now Werner is standing in front of Oma, looking uncertain.

"Talk," I tell them both.

Oma goes first. "Even though you two had that silly fight, he always loved you like a brother."

Werner begins to cry. "He was my best friend."

Oma takes his hands. "Being able to eat your brats again was a joy for him."

"You knew?" I ask.

There is a hint of a smile on Oma's lips. "Who do you think takes out the trash at home?"

I look around the room, at so many friends and family brought together in sadness and joy. This is love.

Ms. Fong, Emmy, and the other paper son friends and relatives are in the lobby near the photo of Lulu in her bridal dress. There are eight of them, not including the kids. In China, eight is a lucky number.

I join the group. "I want to show you something," I tell them.

Chapter 77

The office won't fit us all at once. This is probably the biggest single gathering of Asians Last Chance has ever seen. Everyone wants to look at the paper sons wall. There's Ms. Fong's grandfather looking serious in a faded photo. Henry Sui finds an old Christmas card with a three-cent stamp his uncle sent.

Jolly old Marty Woo, who looks like he's tucked away lots of bao in his lifetime, points to the photo of a young man struggling to hold a rice bag over his head. "That's me!" He pats his belly. "I may have put on a couple pounds since then."

Emmy thinks that a couple of the people on the wall are ones that she's been trying to track down. I point out the photo of Jean Lee and she gasps. Everyone is taking photos of the photos and talking excitedly.

It's like we're having a family reunion right here in the kitchen of the Golden Palace. If you didn't know better, you'd think the Lucky 8, as they've nicknamed themselves, have known each other all their lives. I remember that Oma once said that food, like people, "can be familiar and unexpected at the same time."

When Daisy wanders back to get more shrimp fried rice, she gives me a quizzical look.

"Relatives?"

I nod.

"Your grandfather always said I should be on the wall."

"He did?" I ask.

"Because of my name, I think," she says.

I'm confused. "Daisy?"

"Daisy's my first name. My last name is Gluck. It used to be Glücklich, but my grandparents shortened it when they came to America. My mother told me it means 'lucky' in German."

Chapter 78

I return to the dining room. Oma is still deep in conversation with Werner.

Eva makes her way up to me. "Are you and your mom going to stay in Last Chance?"

I shake my head. "School's going to start soon, and we really should go home."

She squeezes my arm. "I'm going to miss you, Maizy."

"I'm going to miss you, too, Eva."

Logan is circulating, making sure everyone has enough food. Mom is being gracious, accepting the kind words that keep coming at her. I pull her aside and reach into the fishing vest. "From Opa," I tell her.

She trembles when she reads the fortune out loud. "'Charlotte, you are the best daughter a man could have. You make me proud.'"

That day Opa asked me to bring the typewriter home, we wrote fortunes together. He said that I should pass them out when the time was right.

"When is that?" I asked.

"You'll know," he said.

The Noisy Family is silent with awe when Werner does tricks using Opa's playing cards. The mood in the room has slowly turned from funeral to festive and people begin to share their stories about Opa and the Golden Palace. When the Last Chance locals hear about the Lucky 8, everyone wants to talk to them. It's like they're celebrities. Soon people are swapping stories about when and how their own ancestors came to America.

Lady Beth and Marty Woo both claim to recognize each other from decades ago. He's sharing photos of his great-grandchildren. Lady Beth is smiling, something I'm not used to seeing. It looks good on her. She invites his entire family to her house, and he accepts.

Just like that, the world has turned upside down.

I slip Werner a fortune cookie. I'm afraid he may start to cry again, but instead he releases a big, boisterous laugh like I've never heard before.

His fortune reads: So what if I cheated at poker? Just try to get your money back now!

"Is it going to be strange here without him?" I ask my grandmother.

Oma is quietly observing the celebration.

"It already is." Her voice is sad and happy at the same time. "Running the Golden Palace together was the longest honeymoon in history."

I place something in her hand.

Despite everything, my grandfather had always hoped he'd get well. Still, Opa dictated a fortune for his bride, "just in case."

Oma cradles the foil-wrapped cookie.

"From Opa," I tell her.

"Opa?" When she reads the fortune, I can't tell if she is laughing or crying, or both. "That silly old man. I could never stay mad at him."

Sweet and sour.

Yin and yang.

Oma uses Opa's handkerchief and dabs her tears. Her fortune reads:

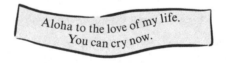

Aloha to the love of my life.
You can cry now.

Later, I make my way around the Golden Palace and pass out more cookies. Love, live, laugh, and eat Chinese food! they say—a quote from my grandfather, of course.

When the basket is empty, I feel empty, too. I reach into my pocket to steady myself. Among the poker chips is something unfamiliar. I open the velvet box and stare at the fancy gold key. Tears begin to flow. Opa must have slipped it into the fishing vest. But when? How?

Inscribed inside the box are these words: *The key to Last Chance, Minnesota, presented to Lucky Chen on his 100th birthday.*

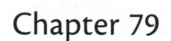

Chapter 79

On our last day before heading back to Los Angeles, Oma calls Mom and me into the office. She's putting an old photo up on the wall. "Another paper son," she explains.

My mother leans in to look at the photo. "This can't be!"

Oma nods. "It is, Charlotte. You are the descendant of a paper son."

I don't understand. "I thought Lucky was here legally," I say.

"Lucky wasn't a paper son." Oma points to the photo. "But my father was one. My sister and I were never allowed to talk about our family secret." She looks at Mom. "Your grandfather, Gung Gung, lived in fear that we'd all be deported."

I remember that Emmy told me about this.

Now Oma looks at me. "Maizy, my father, your great-grandfather, was a paper son. Since you're doing paper son research, you may as well start here. Every story has two sides, and so does every family."

Chapter 80

I t's early in the morning. Mom wants to get on the road soon. While Oma helps her pack the Honda, I take one final walk around Last Chance and stop in front of the Golden Palace.

"Bud," I say. "I'm going to miss you."

Lazy Dog is sleeping nearby. I hug Bud the Bear. "I'll be back," I promise. Upon hearing this, Lazy Dog raises his head, wags his tail, and then closes his eyes again.

I continue my walk, past Ben Franklin and Werner's Wieners. When I near the train depot, I can't help but smile.

"Logan!" I shout, and run toward him.

He's riding circles around the stone well. Worm buckets hang off the back of his bike.

"Maizy! I thought you already left."

"Soon." I point to the well. "You making a wish?" He nods. "What is it this time?" I ask.

His eyes begin to water. "I was wishing that you won't forget about me."

"Oh, Logan," I say. "I could never forget about you. We're always going to be friends."

"You promise, Maizy?"

"I promise."

He grins, then blows his nose on his T-shirt. I'm watching Logan pedal away when he shouts over his shoulder, "Bye, Chinese American Maizy from Los Angeles!"

On my first day in Last Chance, I made a wish. It didn't come true—at least that's what I thought back then. "I wish I were home," I had said into the wishing well.

What I realize now is that I've been home all summer.

Chapter 81

On the day Mom and I got back to Los Angeles, this email was waiting for me:

Dear Maizy,

I heard from one of the Lucky 8 about your search. Decades ago, my great-grandfather found his way to Last Chance. Lucky and Lulu Chen gave him shelter and a job, but more than that, they gave him hope. For that, our family is eternally grateful.

I know a young Chinese American woman who's graduating from culinary school in San Francisco. Her ultimate goal is to run a restaurant. Susie Ling is the daughter of immigrants. I'll tell her about the Golden Palace.

All best,
Elinor Tan, great-granddaughter of
Charlie Tan, Last Chance paper son

I've been in Los Angeles for a few months now. It's so great to be with Ginger. Emmy and I are in touch all the time. She's like a big sister. Lucky and the Golden Palace brought people together through food and friendship. I'm working on bringing people together, too. Emmy's helping me create a Last Chance Paper Sons website. The goal is to connect generations past and present. It's been slow getting started, but that's okay. I have time.

I finally did get my replacement phone. Logan used his worm money to get one, too. He says that now and then Riley eats lunch with him at school, and that his popularity is on the rise. Lady Beth still dines at the Golden Palace every day. Sometimes Finn eats with her and she insists he take home the leftovers. Werner is retiring to Boston to be with his daughter and new grandson. And Daisy is in charge of the town recycling program.

I used to think that Last Chance was the most boring place on the planet. But once I gave the town a chance, its people and stories opened up to me. Take Riley and Lady Beth, for example. At first I thought I knew who they were based on what they looked like on the outside—when really, it's the inside that matters most.

Erik Fisk's friends couldn't keep a secret. Eventually the

whole town knew that it was his idea to steal Bud and leave the racist note. When Erik's mother made him apologize to Oma, he put on a big smile to charm her.

"I won't press charges," Oma assured Erik. Then she smiled back at him and added, "Although the statute of limitations is seven years. Which means, you'd better behave . . . or I could change my mind."

And then there's Mayor Whitlock.

I believed he was a good man, but he wasn't. He didn't have a badge, like the officer who framed Lucky, or a gun, like the men who tried to run Lucky out of Last Chance. But Mayor Whitlock had something just as dangerous. He had words, and he used them to deceive.

Mayor Whitlock has resigned from politics and no longer writes for *Minnesota Dontcha Know*. Apparently, the magazine got an anonymous letter questioning the authenticity of one of his articles. After an internal investigation, he was fired for ethical violations. Later, a Minnesota newspaper ran a story about what he did. I guess Mayor Whitlock's article made him famous after all.

I look out my bedroom window at the palm trees and the Hollywood sign. Tonight, Mom's cooking sizzling ginger beef with broccoli and shrimp fried rice. We're going to make the cream cheese wontons together. Later, we'll video chat with Oma. She got a new computer, and Principal Holmes taught her how to use it.

I think about Opa and his stories all the time. I miss him

every day. Lucky is always on my mind, too. I know that over 150 years have passed since he arrived in America, but some things haven't changed as much as I wish they had.

"There's still lots of work to be done," my grandfather once said.

If he were here right now, I'd tell him, "Opa, I'm ready to go to work."

As for Bud, that bear's been attacked, shot at, kidnapped, painted on, and who knows what else? But he's still standing guard in front of the Golden Palace. And even though I'm not in Last Chance, I feel like I'm right there next to him.

"Tell Bud I said hi!" I say into the phone. I take Lucky's key out of the box to admire it. Mom says we can get it framed, but I like to hold it.

"Tell him yourself," Logan answers in that bossy tone of his. "Hey, when you're back at spring break, will you teach me to play poker?"

"Sure, but prepare to lose," I say.

"Maizy, dinner!" Mom yells.

I put the key back, for now. "I gotta go," I tell Logan. "It's time to eat."

Epilogue

Aloha, Maizy,

I was sitting on the beach thinking about your grandfather. "Old man," I shouted into the waves, "send me a signal if you're with me right now." And just then a double rainbow appeared!

Love,
Oma

P.S. The Golden Palace is in such great hands with Susie Ling and Daisy running it, I may never go back. Instead, maybe I'll move in with you and your mom. What do you think of that?

Author's Note

When I began writing Maizy's novel, the news was overrun with heartbreaking reports about the struggles immigrants faced while trying to come to America. Many were willing to risk their lives to build a better future for their families. That got me thinking about my own family.

Like Maizy's story, mine began in China, a country I've never been to. I'm a third-generation Chinese American, and I grew up in the Los Angeles suburb of Monterey Park.

Me at around Maizy's age

My parents, Marylin and Frank Yee, in the late 1950s

My mom and dad were teachers. When I was very small, my mother's parents took care of me while they were at work.

Po Po and Gung Gung (Cantonese for "Grandma" and "Grandpa") were both born in China in 1900 in Taishan, Canton—now known as Guangdong Province. They had an arranged marriage and wed at the age of eighteen. My grandfather came to the United States in the early 1920s. My grandmother joined him later.

Gung Gung in the 1920s   *Po Po, seen here in China, 1926*

Po Po and Gung Gung and their children.
My mother is at the bottom right.

When I was young, we used to go to my grandparents' house every Sunday. There, my brother, Roger, and I would play with our many cousins while all the aunties and uncles caught up with one another. Food was plentiful and always included the fried wontons Po Po taught me how to make.

In college, I took a class called "The Chinese in America." For the first time, I learned about the hardships and prejudice immigrants from China endured. My grandparents

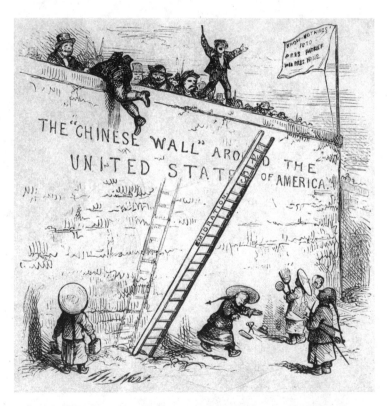

When Chinese immigrants arrived in the United States, they were often met with prejudice, as seen in this editorial cartoon published in Harper's Weekly, *July 23, 1870.*

never spoke about that. Instead, they focused on the good things, like when they became American citizens.

Los Angeles is a melting pot. When I was growing up, no one stared at me because of the way I looked. Later, when I moved to an area where there were few Asians, suddenly total strangers would ask, "Where are you from?" I'd reply, "Los Angeles," and they'd say, "No, what country are you from?" Before this, I hadn't thought much about being Chinese. It was just who I was.

This and other parts of my life began finding their way into Maizy's story.

Though this book is set in the present, it really begins in 1853 with Lucky Chen. Maizy's story and Lucky's, along with Last Chance, the Golden Palace, and the characters in these pages, are works of fiction. This gave me a chance to explore what might have become of someone who traveled from China, endured blatant prejudice and racism while working on the railroads, and then ended up in America's heartland. So often we see the United States' history as facts from textbooks, where the contributions of immigrants are little more than footnotes. I wanted to view it through the lens of the Chinese immigrants who were not just living American history but affecting and building it.

Up to twenty thousand Chinese workers labored on the western part of the transcontinental railroad, known as the Central Pacific, from 1863 through 1869. They made up 90 percent of the labor force and were paid 30 to 50 percent less than their white counterparts.

This image of a young railroad worker is how I imagine Lucky.

Once the transcontinental rail line was complete, the trip across the United States took a week, rather than a month, as it had in the past. It opened up the western part of the country, which most people had heard about but never seen, and provided new economic opportunities for businesses and manufacturers. However, the transcontinental railroad also changed the country in destructive ways. Many trains crossed through tribal lands, destroying Indigenous communities and cultures, altering the landscape and resources, and bringing unwanted white settlements.

For the Chinese arrivals, their place in American history was still being defined. One of the basics of life—food—became a foundation for many to start anew. Canton Restaurant, one of the first documented Chinese restaurants in the United States, opened in 1849 in San Francisco. The Chinese Exclusion Act of 1882 limited the number of Chinese laborers coming to America, with an exception for merchants. In

An early Chinese restaurant in San Francisco, around 1880

1915, restaurant owners were included in that category, and more Chinese restaurants began appearing in areas that didn't have them previously. According to an industry research organization, by 2020, there were more than twenty-five thousand Chinese restaurants in the United States. That tops the number of McDonald's and Burger King restaurants combined!

Chefs work in a restaurant in
one of New York City's Chinatowns in the 1940s.

My research took me to San Francisco, where I explored Chinatown, ate lots of Chinese food, and stopped by the same fortune cookie factory that I had been to when I was a child. Some say fortune cookies first appeared in nineteenth-century Kyoto, Japan. Others claim the first one was spotted in San Francisco in the early 1900s, and there's another contingent that insists they were created in Los Angeles.

While in Minnesota, I visited quaint small towns. The Northfield Historical Society is housed in the bank famous for the 1876 shoot-out between bank robber Jesse James's gang and the townsfolk. That battle found its way into Lucky's legacy.

In writing *Maizy Chen's Last Chance*, I took liberties with other characters and events as well, including the story of actress Jean Lee. Though she is completely made up, I imagined she looked like the "first Chinese American movie star," Anna May Wong.

By the 1880s, 25 percent of California's workers were Chinese. Thousands, like Lucky, had arrived before the Chinese Exclusion Act of 1882. It was the first national law to restrict the immigration of a specific ethnic group.

When the San Francisco earthquake and fires of 1906 destroyed citizenship records, it made it easier for young

Chinese men to purchase fictional identity papers. These "paper sons" claimed they were the children of people of Chinese descent born in the United States. That was the only way Chinese could be citizens at this time—and it made them citizens as well.

Like Maizy's oma, some elderly Chinese American citizens still remember the fear of deportation and don't speak about their paper sons history. My own maternal grandparents came through the Angel Island Immigration Station in San Francisco. My grandfather ran produce sections in small grocery stores. Later, my grandmother worked in a sewing factory, becoming one of the first Chinese women there to join a union.

In Lucky's stories, I wrote about some of the barriers, violence, and slurs that were used against the Chinese immigrants. Sadly, much of the same hostilities and racist language is still around today. It is hurtful and jarring, and I debated how much I should include in this book. Ultimately, I decided to bring a few instances to light and not to shy away from reality.

As I was finishing the final chapters of Maizy's story, hate crimes against Asian Americans were on the rise. I was torn apart and wondered, "What can I do?" Then I told myself—keep writing.

There are some who seek to tear us apart, while others bring people together. I look at Maizy as a bridge, and this book is a tribute not just to Chinese American immigrants but to all who have helped build America. Maizy connects people, places, and even generations. Like most immigrant families, my grandparents sacrificed so much for their children, as did my parents. And now with Maizy's story, I hope that I can pass along some Chinese history to my own children and, someday, to theirs.

Oma's Cream Cheese Wontons

In *Stanford Wong Flunks Big-Time*, I shared my grandmother's fried wontons recipe. Though she never made cream cheese wontons, Maizy's grandmother, Oma, did.

The origin of crab rangoon—fried wontons filled with cream cheese, crab, and spices—is unclear. Some say the dish made its first appearance at the 1904 St. Louis World's Fair. Others claim it was created at Trader Vic's restaurant in San Francisco in the 1950s. A cousin of crab rangoon, the Golden Palace's version was straight-up cream cheese wontons—and many say it was invented in Minnesota!

Turn the page for the recipe!

Wait! Ask for an adult's permission and help before you begin. Kitchen appliances and tools are not toys and should only be used with adult supervision.

8 ounces cream cheese

2 stalks of chopped green onions (optional)

1 teaspoon garlic powder

1 tablespoon soy sauce

24 wonton wrappers

1 egg, beaten

oil for deep-frying (deep enough enough to cover one side of wontons)

In a bowl, mix the cream cheese, chopped green onions, garlic powder, and soy sauce.

Place about a heaping teaspoon of the mixture in the center of each wonton wrapper.

Brush the beaten egg around the edges of each wonton wrapper.

Fold each wrapper in half diagonally to make a triangle. Make sure the sides are tightly sealed.

Heat the oil in a pot or frying pan.

Fry the wontons in the hot oil on both sides until they're golden brown.

Remove them from the oil, place on napkins or paper towels to drain oil and cool, then enjoy!

You can also get creative with your own dipping sauces, such as honey, guacamole, sweet and sour, and more.

Resources

Some of the books I read:

Asian Flavors: Changing the Tastes of Minnesota Since 1875 by Phyllis Louise Harris with Raghavan Iyer (Saint Paul, MN: Minnesota Historical Society Press, 2012)

Chinese in Minnesota by Sheri Gebert Fuller (Saint Paul, MN: Minnesota Historical Society Press, 2004)

The Fortune Cookie Chronicles: Adventures in the World of Chinese Food by Jennifer 8. Lee (New York: Twelve, 2008)

San Francisco's Chinatown (rev. ed.) by Judy Yung and the Chinese Historical Society of America (Charleston, SC: Arcadia, 2016)

Shining Star: The Anna May Wong Story by Paula Woo, illustrated by Lin Wang (New York: Lee and Low Books, 2009)

Sweet and Sour: Life in Chinese Family Restaurants by John Jung (Cypress, CA: Yin and Yang Press, 2010)

Places I visited include:

Chinese American Museum (Los Angeles, California)
camla.org

Chinese Historical Society of America (San Francisco, California)
chsa.org

Golden Gate Fortune Cookie Factory (San Francisco, California)
goldengatefortunecookie.squarespace.com

Minnesota History Center (Saint Paul, Minnesota)
mnhs.org/historycenter

Museum of Chinese in America, Collections and Research
Center (New York, New York)
mocanyc.org/collections

Northfield Historical Society (Northfield, Minnesota)
northfieldhistory.org

A few websites for continuing the conversation:

Becoming American: The Chinese Experience
pbs.org/becomingamerican/chineseexperience.html

Building the Transcontinental Railroad: How 20,000 Chinese
Immigrants Made It Happen
history.com/news/transcontinental-railroad-chinese-immigrants

Chinese-Americans in Minnesota
libguides.mnhs.org/chinese-americans

National Geographic for Kids—Save the Earth
kids.nationalgeographic.com/explore/nature/save-the-earth

Acknowledgments

I could not have written *Maizy Chen's Last Chance* without the support, knowledge, and encouragement of those who went on this journey with me.

Anna Pegler-Gordon, professor, James Madison College director, Interdisciplinary Inquiry and Teaching Program; CB Lee, author and authenticity reader; and Audra Ang, Chinese food expert and co-creator of the Museum of Chinese in America's *Sour, Sweet, Bitter, Spicy: Stories of Chinese Food and Identity in America* exhibit—your expertise was invaluable.

Thank you to Kevin Chu from the Collections and Research Center of the Museum of Chinese in America and to John H. Goodman of the National Railway Historical Society. Henry Gowin, you are a hero for driving me all over Minnesota and exploring the sites with me.

For helping bring this book to life and into the hands of readers, kudos to the incredible Random House team, including Barbara Bakowski, Alison Kolani, Christine Ma, Janet Foley, Kristopher Kam, Joey Ho, John Adamo, and Janine Perez. Plus, Adrienne Waintraub, Kristin Schulz,

Emily Duval, Shaughnessy Miller, Erica Stone, Natalie Capogrossi, artist Rebecca Shieh, and designers Sylvia Bi and Andrea Lau.

Polo Orozco, thank you for your dedication and hard work. Shana Corey, editor extraordinaire, you have my heartfelt gratitude for your incredible insights, enthusiasm, and encouragement. And a huge shout-out to my agent, Jodi Reamer, who insisted that this was a story I could and should write.

To my kids—Kait, it was a joy to be able to share the manuscript with you; Benny, your observations were wonderful, as always. Rob, a million thanks for believing in me, cooking those great meals, and marrying me mid-manuscript during the COVID-19 lockdown.

Mom and Dad, I love you so much. This novel is for you. To my grandparents who sailed from China to America over one hundred years ago—your legacies live on. And finally, to my readers, I hope that Lucky's and Maizy's stories may inspire you to find out more about your history, past and present.

LISA YEE is the award-winning author of *Millicent Min, Girl Genius; Stanford Wong Flunks Big-Time; So Totally Emily Ebers; Absolutely Maybe;* and many other books, including the DC Super Hero Girls novel series and numerous American Girl books. Lisa is a third-generation Chinese American. She says, "I wrote *Maizy Chen's Last Chance* as a tribute to my grandparents and to all the immigrants who made the journey to America." Lisa divides her time between Western Massachusetts and Los Angeles.

LisaYee.com
@LisaYee1